Marrying
THE MARINE

THE BRIDES OF HILTON HEAD ISLAND
BOOK 1

D1526450

international bestselling author

SABRINA SIMS MCAFEE

Marrying the Marine
The Brides of Hilton Head Island
Book 1

Cover Design by Niina Cord
Formatting: Inkstain Interior Book Designing
Editor: Jane Haertel

Sabrina Sims McAfee can be contacted via her website:
www.sabrinasimsmcafee.com

For my daughter, Briana.
God truly blessed me when he gave me you,
my beautiful and loving daughter.
You'll forever have my heart.
Love you more,
Mom

Chapter One

BRAYLON WEXLER STEERED HIS HUMMER along the winding road. Listening to the upbeat tempo streaming through the speakers, he marveled at the small town's breathtaking country scenery.

Huge oaks sprouting reddish-orange leaves lined either side of the road. A glistening blue river stretched beyond the grassy mainland to his right. A change in pace was exactly what he needed, he thought, his mind flashing back to the upsetting news he'd received right before leaving his parents' home in Texas.

He flicked the blinkers, signaling a left, and as he rounded the corner he felt his face straining tight. Madison Monroe, his ex, had kept him from what could be the best thing in his life—a son. Madison had showed up on his mother's doorstep right before his departure with a cute three-year-old little boy by her side, claiming Braylon was the father. As far as he was concerned, the precocious kid didn't resemble him in the least bit. But if the paternity test proved he was Drayton's father, then he'd do the honorable thing— provide him with a stable home and love him the way all children deserved.

Braylon rolled the Hummer into the circular driveway of his grandparents' estate and threw the gearshift into park. Taking in the sight of the crimson brick, two-story mansion centered on acres of thick emerald grass, his lips hitched. He zoned in on the river running serenely behind the main house. It'd been so long since he'd visited the coastal area, way too long. He cut the engine.

To the left of the main house a big green welcome bow was mounted to the guest cottage's front door. He guessed that's where he'd stay until his condo became available. His heart warmed from the kind gesture. Then again, knowing his grandmother, she'd try her hardest to keep him there with her for as long as she could.

When he stepped out onto the asphalt, a brisk breeze fanned his bearded face, and a peppery scent of fall leaves permeated his nostrils. As he rounded the rear of his SUV, Adam appeared on the front porch. The butler hastened toward him.

Braylon pressed the button on his key chain to unlock the trunk. As he hooked a hand under the metal to pry open the hatch, a breathless Adam came to a stop beside him. "Mr. Wexler, hold up, sir!" Adam's voice pitched, causing Braylon to pause. He gave a polite smile. "You finally made it back to the Low Country. Let me get your luggage for you, sir," he offered politely.

Braylon smiled. "Adam. My man…it's good to see you." He gave him a bear hug.

"Likewise, sir," Adam concurred, clapping his back.

Releasing Adam, Braylon met the butler's dark gaze. The handsome older gentleman definitely took pride in his job, but Braylon hated when people waited on him. "No offense, Adam, but I'll get my own bags." He hefted a medium-sized suitcase from the trunk, then lowered it to the ground.

Adam grinned. "None taken. Here's your key to the guest cottage, sir."

"Please…call me Braylon."

2

"Will do. Your grandparents should be home in about thirty minutes or so. They decided to take half a day off from the law firm to give you a proper homecoming."

A proper homecoming…I hope they don't make a huge fuss over me like they used to when I came here to visit as a kid. "I have a meeting on Parris Island at one o' clock, so I hope they get here soon." Working as an Agent for the Marines Criminal Investigation Division, he loved his job, and couldn't wait to bust his ass to catch the bad guys.

"I'll call your grandmother to let her know about your meeting. She'd be quite disappointed if she didn't get a chance to see you until evening. I'll be up at the main house if you need anything." Adam bowed his head.

"Thank you. I appreciate it." Braylon hefted his black suitcase and made his way toward the guest cottage. When he entered, a sweet cinnamon fragrance assailed his nostrils. On the counter sat a plate full of assorted fruits, bagels, and huge cinnamon buns drizzled with white icing. If he didn't know any better he'd think that his grandmother, Willa Wexler, had enormous plans to spoil him during his stay.

This place is perfect. The two-bedroom cottage suited him. The family room was centered between the two bedrooms with a magnificent view of the river, and the huge sixty inch television mounted to the wall made him smile. *I can't wait to watch football on that sucker.* Too bad it wasn't winter yet so he could enjoy that Jacuzzi perched on the deck.

Rolling his luggage behind him, he entered the master bedroom. An office tucked in the corner had its own fireplace which would come in handy on those cold winter nights he had to work until the wee hours of the morning. *Hot damn! This is what's happening.*

After Braylon unpacked, he ate a muffin, then showered.

Standing at the foot of the bed buttoning up his dress shirt, he glanced out the window to find a woman out back sitting underneath a huge oak across from his uncle Royce who had Down's syndrome. *Who's that?*

He crossed the room and drew back the drapes to get a better look at her. As he took in the soft, honey complexion of the woman's skin, he swallowed. The glow of the sun beamed down on the silky strands of black hair hanging past her shoulders. Such a pretty lady, he thought, heat filling his body. *Now this is how a brother likes to return home.*

Braylon turned from the window, walked over to the nightstand, and hefted the phone to call the main house.

"The Wexlers' residence," Adam answered.

"Hey, Adam. It's me, Braylon."

"How can I help you, sir? Sorry, I meant to say Braylon."

"I was just looking out the window and happened to notice Uncle Royce outside with a very pretty woman. Who is she?" Braylon turned back toward the window so he could continue watching her.

Adam chuckled. "Her name is Sandella Summers. Your grand-mother hired her a few years ago to help out with your Uncle Royce while they continue running the law firm. Royce has come a mighty long way ever since she's been helping him."

When his grandmother had mentioned Sandella to Braylon he'd just assumed she was a more mature woman. "So that's Sandella? I expected her to be older."

"There's nothing old about Sandella." Adam chortled.

"Thanks. I hope I didn't interrupt you."

"Not at all. I've just finished cooking lunch. I made a big pot of southern seafood gumbo and crab cake sandwiches. When you're ready to eat, just come on up to the main house and I'll fix your plate for you."

"Thanks, but remember what I said earlier. There'll be no waiting on me."

"If you say so, sir. I mean, Braylon."

Braylon chuckled then hung up. He quickly slid his trousers over his hips, zippered them, then shrugged his arms through the sleeves of his blazer. After brushing his hair, he snatched his keys from the dresser, then headed out back to say hello to Royce, and meet the knockout at the same time.

The scent of recently mowed grass permeated Braylon's nose as he strode toward Sandella. "Hello there," he said, coming to a stop behind her.

Startled, she glanced over her shoulder. She tucked her black, long hair behind her ears, then removed her earplugs. When she tilted her head to look up at him, the gleam of the sun kissed the delicate features of her face, and brightened her caramel-colored eyes.

Light flutters gathered in his stomach. Her flawless honey, brown skin looked soft as cotton as she peeped up at him over a set of long black lashes. *She's smoking hot.*

His throat felt dry and he cleared it. "I'm sorry if I startled you, but I thought you heard me approaching."

Sandella removed the bowl of pecans from her lap, placed it on the ground, then pushed herself up from the white blanket to stand. Her long lashes curled when she blinked. "Yes, you startled me, but it's okay." Her voice floated out like a soft caress.

"That's good because I wouldn't want us to get off to a bad start. I'm Braylon," he announced, extending his hand toward her. She stalled before offering him her sweaty, trembling hand. He'd been known to make women nervous before, but not to this extent, he thought, enjoying the soft feel of her delicate skin.

"I'm Sandella," she said, quickly releasing his firm grip. Glancing up at him, she began fidgeting with the pearl necklace draped elegantly around her sexy, slender neck. "It's nice to finally meet you, Braylon. Your grandparents aren't home right now, but they'll be arriving shortly." She placed the bowl of pecans on her hip, then hastened toward Royce as he sat on the ground circling words in a crossword book over by the dock. Yep, he definitely made her nervous for some reason.

Braylon followed Sandella to the edge of the lawn in the direction of the river. "Uncle Royce? How have you been?" he asked, coming to a stop right behind Sandella. Not bothering to look up, Royce's eyes remained planted in his book. Braylon's loins pulled tight as his eyes traveled over Sandella's curvaceous buttocks. *She's fine, too.*

When Sandella turned to face him, the first thing he saw was her soft-looking lips. Lips that sexy had to be tasty. "Willa said that you weren't coming until next week," she said.

Raking his eyes over the lush curves of her figure, something indescribable tugged at his heart. "I guess she forgot to tell you my plans had changed." He'd just met the woman and his lips were dying to mate with hers. "I came a few weeks early so I could get acquainted with the island and Beaufort before reporting to work."

"Oh."

"My grandmother brags on you all the time. She told me how well you work with Royce. She says he's even reading now because of you."

Her cheeks flushed. "I love working with Royce. He's very special to me."

His eyes lowered to the pecans inside the bowl, then back up to her brown, succulent lips. "Grandma Willa tells me you're a great cook. From what she says, everyone loves the caramel pecan pies you bake. Is that what the pecans are for?"

She nodded. "Yes. I make them daily and sell them to the local bakeries, restaurants, and a few hair salons." Her tongue darted over her bottom lips before she sucked it back in.

A naughty vision of him thrashing his tongue with hers entered his mind. He grinned. *I can't wait to sample your pie*, he thought, thinking the sweet pie between her legs was probably just as sweet as the pies she baked.

A discerning look developed in her caramel pupils. "What pie are you talking about?" her tone was accusatory.

My eyes must've said it all. Please don't let her think I'm a jerk, or a pervert. Braylon took pride in honoring and respecting women. After all he had a sister and wouldn't want any man making her feel uncomfortable. In hopes of making the awkwardness stabbing the air vanish, he sought the right words to say. "I'm sorry if I—"

She sighed. "Please don't take this the wrong way," she touched her chest in an endearing manner, "while I appreciate everything the men and women in the service have done for this country, I have a hard time befriending Marines. So if I ever seem abrupt, please don't take it personally," she said.

Well, damn. Her brutal honesty stunned him, made his heart clench. *Her ex-boyfriend must've been a Marine and broken her heart.* "Why's that?"

Shaking her head, the sadness in her eyes grew deeper by the second. Her gaze fell to the ground, then lifted. "I'd rather not talk about it at the moment. Now if you'll excuse me, I have to go prepare Royce's lunch." She reached for Royce's hand, and helped him to stand. Walking hand in hand, they slowly made their way across the lawn back toward the main house.

"I hope you'll tell me all about it, someday." He called after her.

With the hem of her dress blowing around her knees, she glanced back over her shoulder, and gave him a serious stare. Strands of silky black hair brushed against her lips. She turned away.

Braylon's curiosity deepened as he watched her step inside the house and disappear. *I don't know why you feel the way you do about Marines, Sandella. But come hell or high water, I'm going to find out. I'm going to prove to you that not all the Marines here are complete assholes.*

Just as he took a step forward, his grandparents, Drake and Willa, burst through the back door onto the porch. A big smile turned up his grandmother's lips. "You're here!" she shouted, waving. "Come a give your grandma a hug!"

ON MONDAY MORNING, SANDELLA STOOD in the doorway of the Wexlers' mansion waving goodbye to Drake and Willa as they drove off in their silver Bentley, heading for work. Once they were out of sight, she closed the door and headed for the kitchen to make Royce's breakfast.

She pulled open the refrigerator and grabbed a carton of eggs. She then hefted a pint of milk, a bag of sharp cheddar cheese, and a deep dish pastry shell. *Royce loves my ham, egg, and cheese quiche. Maybe I can offer some to Bray—* As soon as the fine specimen Braylon entered her mind, she tried hard to force the extremely gorgeous man right on out. The last thing she needed was to get involved with some man, especially him, a Marine. What did she care anyway? A man like him would never be interested in a plain, inexperienced virgin like her anyhow.

While whisking the ingredients for the quiche together in a green ceramic bowl, her mind traveled back to her first meeting with Braylon on Friday. Regretting how she'd probably made him feel, she released a soft breath. Why had she been so short with him?

All weekend long she'd beaten herself up for opening up and practically admitting to him that she didn't trust the Marines in this area. She'd been a fool, and wrong to say such a thing. Quite honestly, as a whole, she thought very highly of the brave strong men and the courageous women, too.

The whisk stilled inside the bowl. *I made such a fool of myself. Braylon probably thinks I'm discriminatory.* Her problem wasn't with *all* the Marines, just *one* in particular—her mother's rapist and killer. She along with her brothers and father had good reason to believe a Marine had murdered her mother. Unfortunately, till this day, her mother's killer had never been captured. For all she knew, that horrible man might still live in the area, or be working on that darn base. Maybe someday, once he was brought to justice, she'd be able to put the past behind her.

They'll never reopen my mother's case. Never. The pain of her mother's brutal assault threatened to make her cry as if it'd just happened yesterday. As she poured the egg mixture in the pie shell her heart squeezed. She lowered the hatch on the oven and slid the breakfast entree inside.

After pondering over what to do next, she headed to the library to select a heartwarming book to read. Perusing the cherry wood bookshelf inside the antique-filled room, she decided to give a book by Danielle Steel a try. She pulled the hardcover book from the shelf, crossed the room to a window, plopped down on the plush leather couch, and sat reading for nearly an hour.

At the sound of the kitchen buzzer, she lifted her head from the novel. Her eyes spied the clock on the wall. *It's already been an hour*, she thought, heading for the kitchen to remove the breakfast pie from the oven. She'd been so caught up in the book time had flown by.

The scent of the buttery pastry sailed into her nostrils as she placed the hot quiche on top of the stove. *Mmm, Braylon is going to love—*

An image of Braylon's gorgeous, olive-complexioned face and

hazel brown eyes appeared in her mind's eye. Her nipples pulled tight against the pink cotton shirt she wore. How could she have an immediate attraction to someone she'd just met? Worse...how could she let a Marine make her feel such a thing? *Dad would die if he knew of this.*

Her heart flopped as she thought about how her father, Kane, would react if he knew she'd allowed a Marine to make her hot just from merely thinking of him. Her father would kill Braylon if he knew she'd been lusting for him. While she might be leery of the military men surrounding the area, her father downright loathed them.

All these emotions had her in dire need of a walk along the boat dock. She raised a finger to the intercom to call for Royce when, suddenly, he and Adam entered the kitchen.

"Good morning," Adam said with a polite smile on his dark, salt-and-pepper bearded face.

"Good morning Adam. Good morning Royce."

Royce nodded. His voice came out quick when he said, "Hi. Sandy." He rushed over to the dinette table and plopped down in the chair. "Hungry. Eat. Now." He lifted his fork then smiled at her.

"Breakfast is coming right up, Royce," Sandella said.

Adam's eyes landed on the quiche on top of the stove. "That breakfast you made sure looks tasty."

She smiled. "Thanks. Please have some."

"I will do just that. You know I loves your cooking, Sandella." He patted his round belly. "I'm good and hungry, too."

She laughed. "Thanks, Adam. If all the men around town were easy to please like you, maybe I wouldn't be single." She placed a big slice of quiche on a plate for Royce, and then did the same for Adam. She then poured two glasses of freshly made orange juice and handed the drinks to each of them.

Adam took a seat at the table across from Royce. "Well there's a new man in town, a mighty good one if you ask me, and he's been asking about you already."

"Who?" she queried.

His brows hitched. "Why, Willa's grandson, Braylon, that's who. I've known him since he was a baby," his deep voice came out groggy, "and he seems to have grown into a mighty fine young man."

Sandella gave her head a light shake. "Oh no. I'm sure you're misunderstanding. A man like him would never be interested in someone like me."

He pinned her with the strangest look. "And what's wrong with you?"

"I'm too bor—"

Adam's hand flew up, stopping her from uttering another single word. "Stunning." He waggled the fork at her. "Don't say negative things about yourself, Sandella. Not only are you beautiful on the outside, but you're beautiful on the inside, too. Any man would be lucky to have someone like you." He winked. "Any man." Smiling, he forked the food into his mouth.

Flattered by his compliment, she flushed. "You're too kind, Adam. Thanks."

"Don't thank me, it's true. One day you're going to make a mighty fine wife to some lucky man."

She tilted her head. "Ahh. I don't know about that, Adam. Do you mind watching Royce for me while I take a short walk?"

"Of course not."

"Thanks. I won't be long," she said, heading for the dock.

THIRTY-FIVE MINUTES LATER, SANDELLA OPENED the back door to the kitchen. Her heart plummeted past her knees

11

when she spotted Braylon sitting at the table enjoying the breakfast quiche she'd made.

When he looked up from his plate and met her gaze, his face split into a handsome grin. She just about melted. He picked up the napkin lying next to his plate, then swiped it over his handsome mouth. "Good morning."

Anxiety bloomed in her belly as she stepped inside. "Good morning." She shut the door behind her.

"Adam told me it was okay if I helped myself to the quiche you made. I hope you don't mind because it's mighty delicious." He lifted his glass to sip the freshly squeezed orange juice she'd prepared at the break of dawn.

Her body tingled all over. "I'm glad you're enjoying it."

"Why don't you join me?" he asked, pulling out the chair beside him for her to sit.

"Maybe some other time I'll join you, but not right now. I need to go take care of Royce. He's on a strict routine, and gets agitated easily when he gets off track."

He leaned back in the chair. Starting with her eyes, his bright hazel gaze lingered down the length of her body. "You said something on Friday that bothered me the entire weekend."

I made a complete idiot of myself. "Please accept my apology for being so outspoken. I'm normally not like that."

He eyed her speculatively. "No apology needed, Sandella. Things happen," he said, his voice husky. "If you're available later on today, I'd like to take you to lunch at a nice little seafood place on the ocean I heard about. Are you available?"

He's so handsome. And masculine. Braylon's kind offer enticed her. Tempted to say yes, water filled her mouth, forcing her to swallow. "I'm sorry, but I can't. Thanks anyway." Without uttering another word, she hastened out of the kitchen. Mounting the staircase, her hands glided along the black, iron railing. *There's no need to start something you can't finish*, she convinced herself, heading inside Royce's bedroom.

BRAYLON HEARD THE LOUD DRONE of a vacuum cleaner coming from the direction of the library. *Why can't you join me, Sandella?* Her refusal of his invitation disturbed him because it'd been the first time any woman had done such a thing. Jesus Christ. He hoped like hell he wasn't losing his touch. He pushed back his chair, stood, and headed toward the humming noise. Just as he rounded the corner into the dim library with burgundy-painted walls, Adam turned off the vacuum cleaner.

"How's it going this morning, Braylon?" Adam asked, wrapping the cord around the hook.

"My man...you finally stop calling me, sir. Glad it didn't take you long." Braylon held out a fist, and Adam bumped it. Because he wanted information on Sandella, he had to think how to approach the situation.

"Is there anything I can help you with?"

"Yes." He shut the door to ensure some privacy. "I don't know how to ask you this other than to just come out and ask. What's wrong with Sandella?"

"I don't know what you mean."

"Between you and me...she and I had a conversation on Friday that has disturbed me ever since. She said that she doesn't befriend Marines. Was her last boyfriend in the military?" *Why do I even care?*

Adam, old enough to be his grandfather, shook his head. "No. it's nothing like that. The poor girl has been through a lot. I would tell you, but Sandella and I are very close, and the subject has been off limits for many years."

Braylon shrugged. "Something horrible must've happened."

"If you stick around long enough, she just may confide in you. But for the time being, try to get better acquainted with Sandella. She's a mighty fine woman to know."

"Okay. I think I'll do that," Braylon said, admiring the obvious loyalty Adam had for his grandparents as well as Sandella.

With the handle of the vacuum cleaner in his grip, Adam disappeared out into the hallway.

Standing in the center of the library, Braylon's eyes roved over the many rows of books stacked on the shelves. Willa had enough books to open up her own bookstore. His mother had always said that his grandma's constant reading is what had made her so smart.

Sensual thoughts of a pretty Sandella flashed inside his brain. He walked over to the book shelf and pulled a white photo album off the hutch. He flipped to the first page to find a photo of his mother and father smiling on their wedding day. *Mom looks so young and beautiful in this picture. Dad looks buff, and happy.* When he went to replace the album, he spotted a red velvet box to the rear.

Assuming the box held more photos, he grabbed it, then slid the album back on the shelf. He walked over to the chocolate leather couch by the tall bay windows that exposed a beautiful view of the sun shining down on the river. He fell back on the sofa, then kicked off his shoes. He removed the lid on the container, placing it in his lap.

Old newspaper clippings were folded inside the rectangular red box. He reached inside, pulled out a clipping, and unfolded it. His heart grappled at the name printed at the top of the obituary— Sugar Summers.

The woman in the photo had long black hair, soft skin, and was simply beautiful just like Sandella. *This has to be Sandella's mother.* He read the obituary in its entirety confirming it was indeed her mother. *I wonder how she died?*

He placed the paper on top of the lid sitting in his lap, pulled out another newspaper clipping, then unfolded it. *Jesus Christ!* His pulse pounded in his neck after reading the title: **Family Suspects Marine Killed Woman.**

According to the article an arrest was never made. This explained Sandella's uneasiness around him, why she felt the way she did toward the Marines in this part of the country. As he stared blankly at the picture of Sandella's mother, Sugar, he wondered what kind of beast would rape and kill this beautiful woman. *A fucking monster got away with this. A damn monster.*

He neatly refolded both articles, stood, then placed the box back on the shelf behind the photo album where he'd found it. With his heart aching for Sandella's loss, he crossed the room to peer out the window. Knowing a Marine had caused her heartfelt misery, his blood boiled. A man capable of such hideous crimes had no right to be a part of the armed forces. He didn't deserve to carry the name Marine.

Braylon grunted. His fingers flexed by his side as he watched a sailboat cruise to the other side of the river. He detested whoever did this cruel act. Not only had he brought Sandella grief, he'd pained her entirely family and all those that loved both her and Sugar. *I have to show you that you can trust Marines, Sandella. Not all of us are criminals. I need to speak with you.*

Before he turned to go find her, he spotted Sandella pulling close the kitchen's back door. Holding Royce's palm with one hand, she carried a couple of books in the other and began walking along the emerald grass toward the river.

She wore a soft pink top and a pair of light blue denim jeans that fit perfectly over her round butt. The ends of her hair turned up, making Braylon believe it was windy outside. When she turned to look at Royce, he caught a good glimpse of the smile lighting up her face. Royce smiled back at her. *She loves Royce.*

She released Royce's hand and spread a large plaid blanket on the ground underneath the tree. They both sat simultaneously after she handed him a book. She draped an arm over his shoulder. Apparently she was reading to him, or maybe him to her. Sandella's faithfulness to his uncle impressed him.

While Braylon continued to observe her from a distance, he couldn't help but think she was definitely a woman he'd love to become better acquainted with, like Adam had suggested. Maybe they could get to know one another and become friends. *I'd much prefer friends with benefits.* Deep down inside he knew it'd only be a matter of time before he tried to get the sweet-looking princess into his bed and make sweet love to her.

The sight of her was driving him mad with lust. "Oh Sandella. I want you bad, my darling," he murmured. As he thought about how he'd like to flick his tongue over her black nipple his cock twitched.

You deserve a good man in your life. Could I be that man? Not if Drayton is really my son. If he is, I'd have to do the honorable thing, and support his mother, Madison. A rough grumble escaped his lips when Madison came seeping into his brain. While he'd been traveling the country as a CID Agent, rumor had it she'd been unfaithful. And although she'd denied it, he couldn't help but wonder if the accusations were indeed true.

After he and Madison had called it quits three years ago, he'd decided to concentrate his studies on getting promoted up the ranks in the military. His hard-work ethics had paid off, and earned him a position as a Criminal Investigator with the Marines, making him an Agent, or as some civilians liked to say, a detective. While studying and training in the US Army CID Special Agent Course, he'd decided to forgo engaging in any serious relationships.

Of course he'd fucked plenty of women, but that was all it'd been between him and the females, a good fucking. Because he didn't partake in head games, the women had all known that sex was all he'd wanted, and they'd been just fine with giving him just that—great sex.

Now, looking at Sandella, he wondered if he was starting to need more than a fulfilling career to satisfy him. Sure, being a Criminal Investigator for the Marines was rewarding and he wouldn't trade it for the world. But what good was all of that without a woman like Sandella to share it with?

Royce closed the book in his hand, she took it, then they both stood. She gathered her belongings, and turned facing the window. As she made her way back up to the main house, she caught him staring at her. A light smile touched her succulent lips. His heart stirred, and his lance hardened like fucking steel.

I want you, and I'm going to have you.

Chapter Two

SANDELLA LOWERED ROYCE'S PLATE CONTAINING pita bread stuffed with rotisserie chicken and a side of plain Lay's chips to the table. She returned to the counter to wipe up the tiny crumbs from the peanut butter crackers he'd enjoyed earlier. As she circled the cloth over the marble countertop, she heard footsteps coming up behind her. *Braylon?* Her body tensed.

Earlier that morning she'd noticed him looking at her through the bay window from inside the library. His bold stare had sent chills skittering up her spine, and she couldn't help but wonder why he'd looked at her like that. *Was he interested in her? No. That couldn't be it. He was simply enjoying the scenery out back.*

From behind her, someone cleared his throat. "Excuse me, Sandella." Braylon's baritone voice made her arms dot with goose bumps.

"Yes?" she said, turning. When her gaze met his, a tingle rushed to her center. Although she'd never had sex with a man before, Braylon's dominating presence pulled her to him like a powerful magnetic field, electrically charging her body. *I have to stop this.*

"Do you by any chance know where Adam is? I need to speak with him." His voice threatened to strike a fire inside her.

You're so good looking. "He's out front, trimming the hedges."

"Although you turned down my offer earlier, I hope you'll reconsider joining me. If you don't want to go out, maybe we can spend some time together right here on the estate."

"I think it's best if we don't—"

"I promise if you give me just a few minutes of your time," his handsome face widened with a buttery smile, "I'll try my hardest to make it worth your while. Will you at least think about it?" He stepped closer, limiting the space between them.

She craned her neck to look up at him. Heat spooled inside his titillating hazel gaze. *His lips are so sexy.*

She started to perspire and her fitted jeans felt like sheaths of clammy cloth. She nodded. "Yes, Braylon. I'll think about it," she said, already knowing her answer was yes.

"Good. Talk to you later." He turned and headed toward the living room to exit through the front door, leaving her burning with desire.

SANDELLA ROLLED HER FORD TAURUS into the driveway of her father's house where she lived. Her small, wooden home was the epitome of Lowcountry living. Burly oaks spiraling with grey moss rooted in her front yard, and colorful fall leaves lay scattered on the grass, browning at the edges. Flanked with black shutters around the windows, the white three-bedroom home was located in Beaufort, close to Parris Island military base.

Sluggish from working all day, she clambered up the wooden steps. The unstable worn boards creaked beneath her feet with every step she took until she reached the porch. Starting with the chipped paint on the window frames, her home certainly needed a makeover. But when did she ever have the time to do anything other than take care of Royce and her youngest brother, Drew?

Exhausted, she released a breath. She hooked a hand on the silver metal of the screen door and pulled it open. When she stepped inside the living room the freezing temperature submerged her. *Why does he keep it so cold in here?* She shivered.

"Is that you, Sandy?" her father, Kane, yelled from the small family room just off the kitchen.

Easing the strap of her purse from her shoulder, she confirmed, "Yes, Dad. It's me." She placed her purse and keys on the kitchen counter, then turned the stove on high.

Kane rolled inside the room, sitting in his wheelchair. With his hands on the wheels, he looked up at her. "About time you got home. I tell you, Sandy, I think Willa works you too damn hard, and long. Reminds me of how they used to work the shit out of your mother. I think you need to look for—"

She tilted her head. "I'm not looking for another job, Dad. I love what I do. Besides, Willa pays me great money to take care of Royce. There's no way I could find another job around here making the kind of money she and Drake pays me." *Especially without having a degree.* Thank God, she only had one more year before graduating with her Bachelor's online.

"Well, keep working for them then," Kane coughed, the sound of mucus rattling in his throat. "I'd die if you ever left Beaufort." He patted his chest. "Just die."

Sandella giggled. "Stop saying that, Dad."

Angst rounded his deep chocolate eyes. "Well it's true, dog, own it. I just love you so much. You gone always be my baby girl, and it'll just kill me if you ever leave me." With his elbow resting on the arm of his wheelchair, he curved a finger over his mustache. Ever since the car accident had left him paralyzed from the waist down he'd become very dependent on her, but she didn't mind doing whatever she could for him. She loved him. "Just breaks my heart thinking about it. You look every bit of your mother, my Sugar."

"Ahhh, Dad. Stop looking so sad." Ever since her mother had been murdered, Kane had become extremely overprotective of her and her brothers, but especially her. Her brothers felt their father sheltered her way too much. Often she had to remind them that she was fine with her life just the way it was. Besides, they had some nerve to talk. At times they were just as overprotective.

She placed the marinated pork chops in the heated frying pan and began sautéing them in olive oil. She turned away from the meat and faced her father again. "You know, Dad…I just might find me a man and get married someday." Kane's brows gathered in the center of his forehead. "Then you'll have no choice but to let me go."

Kane wheeled his chair as close as he could get to her. "I guess you're right," he grumbled, glaring up at her. He frowned. "But I tell you what…any man you marry better be worthy of my only daughter, and he better treat you right. Because if he don't, he might end up with a bullet in his goddamn back!" His voice escalated, meaning every single word.

She leaned over and gave her father's forehead a peck. "Is smothered pork chops with yellow rice and green beans okay for dinner?"

"How many times do I have to tell you that whatever you fix for dinner is okay with me? You don't ever have to cook again another day in your life as far as I'm concerned. Lord, girl, you work hard just like your momma, my sweet Sugar, used to."

Her heart warmed inside her chest as she remembered her mother's hard work ethics. "I don't mind cooking. It's important to me that you and Drew get a good meal every day." She slid her hand in the back pocket of her jeans, retrieved a black elastic band,

and pulled her hair into a tight ponytail. "Where's Drew?"

"He's in his bedroom doing his homework. He wanted to go to the community center and play football, but I told him to get his work done first."

"That reminds me, I need to go online and check his grades."

"He's gone be grounded if they're bad is all I'm gone say." Kane rolled his chair to the other side of the kitchen, picked up his carton of cigarettes, and lit one. "Call me when dinner's ready." Puffing on the cigarette, he wheeled out of the kitchen.

God, I wish he'd stop smoking. Sandella poured brown gravy over the pork chops. While the green beans simmered in bacon and onion inside the pot on the stove, she decided to go check on her baby brother, her heart, Drew.

As she walked down the dull narrow hallway toward Drew's bedroom, a vision of Braylon's masculine face and full sexy lips invaded her mind. She really wanted to accept his invitation to go out on a date with him, but the point would be moot. Her father would never in a million years accept her relationship with him. Because of the strong, close relationship she had with her overbearing dad, she had to find a man that he'd accept.

Growing frustrated over the thought, she huffed. *Braylon wouldn't stand a chance with Dad. Because of what happened to Momma, he despises Marines. He'd probably disown me. Or die of heartbreak. If I accepted Braylon's date, he'd feel like I betrayed the family.*

Sorrow dredged up inside her heart as she rounded the corner into Drew's room. Drew sat on the bed with his legs crossed, surrounded by thick textbooks. Admiring his studious behavior, she smiled, then entered. "Hey there...how was your day?" She lowered herself next to him on the bed.

Drew peered up at her then back down at his homework. "I'm just trying to figure out this math problem. Dang, Sandy...this mess is hard." He bit down on the eraser of his pencil.

"Let me take a look at the problem." She hefted the algebra textbook into her lap. "What number?"

"Number thirteen."

At first the problem on the page looked foreign to her, but finally she was able to show him how to do it. Now that all of his homework was complete, he smiled. "Thanks, Sandy." Drew jumped off the bed, pulled back the door of his closet, and grabbed his football from the shelf.

She stood, fists on hips. "And where do you think you're going?"

"I'm going to play football at the community center." Drew shuffled the football in his hands. "Bye." He hastened out the room, down the hallway, toward the front door.

"Come back before it gets dark," she said, following him.

With his football still in his hand, Drew dashed past Kane as he sat on the front porch smoking his lungs away. "Where do you think you're going?" he asked Drew as the boy descended the steps. "Stop right there, goddamn it!"

Drew stopped dead in his tracks when his feet hit the ground. He turned to face his father. "Sandy said I could go and play football as long as I come back before dark."

"You're not going anywhere. Now get back in the house. I'm the daddy, and what I say goes," Kane grumbled.

Sandella knew Kane's reasoning for not wanting Drew to go had everything to do with the company he kept. He hated the fact that his closest friends' fathers and mothers were in the Marines. Something had to give. After meeting Braylon, she'd had even more of a change of heart.

Here we go. A loud squeak resounded through the air when Sandella pushed the screen door open. Holding on to the frame, she glanced down at her father. "He's finished with his homework,

Dad. Please...let him go."

Pinning Drew with a harsh glare, Kane rubbed circles over his beard. "Lord Jesus. My own daughter barking rules like she's the parent. What is this world coming to?"

Drew's mouth broke into a smile. "So can I go? Please, Dad, please."

Kane took a long slow drag of his cigarette, then blew the smoke out through his nose. "Go ahead and go, boy. But if those thugs start talking all that nonsense about you joining the Marines again, you better bring your behind home. And I better not catch you visiting none of them Marines' houses, either. Do you understand?"

Sandella sighed. It'd been a year since Drew had been caught over at Lieutenant Miller's home and her father still felt the need to bring it up every other day. "He knows that, Dad."

Drew tossed the ball up in the air then caught it. "Don't worry. I won't listen to anything those idiots have to say!" He beamed with excitement. "I'm not going to be a Marine. I'm going to be a lawyer just like Drake Wexler!" He took off running down the street.

Kane slapped his thigh. "Hot damn...now we're talking!" Chortling, he slid the cigarette butt back between his chapped lips.

The mere mention of all this military stuff caused Braylon's name to linger around the edges of Sandella's mind. Turning blindly, she bumped into the door and stumbled.

"Watch out there now!" Kane's voice rose. "Are you okay?"

"I'm fine, Dad. Just peachy keen." She straightened her stance. *I'd be even better if you stopped criticizing Marines all the time.* She opened the door and heard the timer on the stove bleeping. *The Mexican corn bread is ready.* She glanced back over her shoulder. "Dinner is ready whenever you are."

As she made her way into the kitchen sensual thoughts of the fine Braylon flooded her mind. He'd looked as handsome as ever when he'd smiled at her at the table this morning. His cologne had smelled rich, like oranges and pines. The thin fabric shirt he'd worn had revealed the solid muscles of his ripped chest.

Sandella pulled a plate from the cupboard and sighed. *I think I'm going to be in trouble if I keep hanging around Braylon.* Although he was away in Hilton Head, he had a serious effect on her brain.

HEAVY FOG SATURATED THE MORNING air, making it difficult for Sandella to see as she drove along the winding road leading to the Wexlers' estate. She flicked on her bright lights, then changed the station from light sounds to an urban station. A pretty love song by Jennifer Hudson filled her ears, sending her to thoughts to Braylon.

Nibbling her bottom lip, she imagined him kissing her. *I have to stay away from him.* As good as he looked he probably was a two-timing playboy.

She pulled up in the driveway, then brought the car to a complete stop. Ready to start her day, she opened the car door. Just as her feet hit the pavement, the front door flung open, and Willa came running out the house toward her.

Thinking something horrible had happened, Sandella's stomach knotted. *Dear God, I hope no one died.* She hurried up the length of the driveway and met Willa halfway.

Breathing erratically, Willa palmed Sandella's shoulders. "Let me," she swallowed, "catch my breath." Her big boobs heaved up and down.

As Willa stood grappling for her next breath, Drake stalked outside carrying two suitcases. "Go get your purse, Willa. I don't have all day." He came to a stop in front of them.

"Don't rush me." She rolled her eyes at Drake. "This is the third time your mother has pretended to be dying!"

Drake looked heavenward. "She's not pretending this time, Willa. Fred said she's really sick. They even had to take her to the hospital."

"I wouldn't be surprised if her mean behind died and came back," Willa snapped. She then directed her attention back to Sandella. "Anyway, Sandella, darling...I have a big favor to ask of you."

"Just name it, Willa."

"Drake's mother is terribly ill. If it's not a bother, I need you to stay here with Royce until we get back from North Carolina."

Sandella's eyes honed in on the guest cottage where Braylon was probably sleeping. Suddenly, a light clicked on in his bedroom. *Oh God, no. I can't be alone with him.* "I don't mind keeping Royce overnight, but if it's okay with you, I'd like to take him back to my house."

Shaking her head wildly, Willa threw her hands up. "No offense, Sandella. But he hates going to your house, or anybody's house for that matter. Remember what happened the last time he went home with you? He and your father both had a hissy fit."

"But, but, but I think it'll—"

Willa grabbed her wrist, and slapped a wad of cash in her opened hand. "That's a little bonus for your troubles. Thanks," she said, gently patting her cheek.

Sandella spied the several one-hundred-dollar bills lying in her palm. "Willa, this is too much. You don't have to pay me anything extra."

"Oh, yes I do." She put her mouth to Sandella's ear and through clenched teeth whispered, "If that old bat pulls the same little stunt she did last time, God only knows how long it'll take Drake to realize his mother is playing him for a fool. The woman loves attention."

"Stop talking and go get your purse," Drake muttered, easing into the Bentley behind the steering wheel.

"Okay, okay, okay. I'm hurrying." Willa rushed back inside the house to grab her purse and quickly returned to where Sandella was still standing, baffled. "Oh yeah, by the way, don't forget Adam's three-week vacation started today."

That's right, Adam's gone too. Sandella's mouth parted then snapped shut. "So I'll be here with Braylon all by myself?" *The fine Marine.*

Willa's lips curved upward. "Yes, you will. Braylon is as sweet as they come, darling. He won't bother you at all. And if you need anything he'd be more than willing to oblige." Willa patted her shoulder.

Drake cranked the engine. The passenger side window rolled down. "Let's go, Willa!" he bellowed. "You're taking your sweet time as if my mother isn't important."

"Call me if you need me." Willa jumped in the car and shut the door.

Sandella stood in the center of the curved driveway watching the Bentley drive off into the thick, unrelenting fog. Finally, the red taillights disappeared into the early morning darkness. She turned on her heels, and as she strode toward the house, the guest cottage's door flung open.

Braylon stepped out onto the porch, shirtless. "Is everything out here okay?" he questioned, stalking toward her like a tall fearless knight, fog rustling against the flexed muscles of his bare flesh.

Her heart clenched as he closed in on her. Overwhelmed by his powerful presence, her knees weakened. She bowed her head, looking at the cold concrete. *We're going to be all alone indefinitely. Oh boy.*

His bare feet came to a stop in front of her. She'd always heard men with big feet had giant private parts. Desire coursed through her veins like boiling liquid.

Starting with his feet, her gaze slowly traveled up the length of his body, then clung to the deep cuts on his firm, beefy torso.

Tempted to reach out and touch his beaded nipples, her hand itched with hot need. Considering she'd never been with a man before, her sensual desire for him surprised her.

"An emergency came up with Drake's mother so he and Willa had to leave. She said she didn't want to wake you and she'd call later to fill you in."

"Oh, I see. Grandma told me yesterday that Adam was going on vacation so it's just you, me, and Royce. Have you given any more thought to that date I asked you on?"

"Umm. Well—"

He touched a finger to her chin, tilting her head. His hazel eyes glittered. Chemistry sizzled between them. "I'm glad you decided to take me up on my offer. You and Royce be ready by twelve," he stated, answering for her.

Braylon's take-charge attitude and constant persistence turned her on. Saliva gathered in her mouth. *Kiss me. Kiss me.* "Okay." Like a schoolgirl with her first crush, she whirled and practically scuttled for the main house. When she reached the doorway, she turned, and then paused, taking in his dominating physique.

As the ball of morning sun rose behind the oaks, the wispy fog surrounding Braylon started to dissipate. Smiling, he said, "I could move inside the main house with you until they get back, if you want me too."

Oh God, no! "No thanks. I'll be fine," she said, slamming the door by accident. With her back slumped against the heavy wooden door, she draped an arm over her forehead to collect her frenzied thoughts. *Left here with a Marine, a fine one at that...why is this happening?*

Her father's deep voice charged into her brain, causing her jaws to tighten. He'd once said, "I hope you use the sense that God gave you...*never* get involved with a damn Marine. They're rapists and rotten-ass dogs, Sandy." Kane had said the ill words on too many occasions for her to even count.

With Kane's voice ringing over and over inside her head, she ascended the staircase. Reaching the top, she turned left, and headed inside Royce's room.

Sandella smiled down at Royce as he lay in bed on his side with his eyes closed. She grazed his freckled cheeks with her knuckles. "Time to get up, sleepyhead."

Royce stirred and his eyes fluttered open. He stretched long arms and legs beneath the navy comforter, then sat upright. He yawned. "Morning time!" He flung his feet to the floor and scurried inside the bathroom.

While Royce was in the bathroom, she made the bed. After placing the big fluffy pillows against the headboard, she walked over to the oblong mirror sitting in front of the window. "Who are you?" she asked herself, realizing she hadn't been living. Of course she was alive, but alive and living were two different things.

Her brothers, Aric, Chandler, and Drew, had been right. She'd lived under her father's control for way too long, had distanced herself from every man in the area because he'd ordered her to do so. It was high time she stopped acting as if she was Daddy's little girl and behaved like the adult woman she was. Things were about to change. So whether Kane liked it or not, she was going to go out with Braylon and make an effort to enjoy herself. After everything she'd given up to raise her brothers, she deserved to finally have some fun.

She observed her plain face without any makeup and her simple appearance in the mirror. *Braylon seems mighty, mighty fun. Maybe I should try spicing myself up a little.*

After Royce brushed his teeth, he walked over to the chair next to the mirror and sat. "Finished," he said, wringing his hands in his lap.

"Let's see," she said, pulling open the accordion doors of his closet. "You and I have a date today so we have to look nice."

Royce smiled. "Date. Date."

"Yes. We have a date with your nephew Braylon."

"Br…Br.." Royce attempted to but couldn't quite get the words out.

"Braylon." She lay a white Polo shirt and a pair of navy jeans on the bed for him. "When you're finished dressing, comb your hair, and come downstairs for breakfast."

Royce said, "I like clothes."

"I'm going downstairs to do the laundry." She left the room, smiling, and wondered where Braylon was taking them for lunch.

After Sandella separated the laundry, she stood at the stove whisking batter for the red velvet pancakes Royce always thoroughly enjoyed. Although Royce was a grown man, and was far older, he seemed more like a brother to her. Probably because Willa treated her like a daughter.

She removed the nonstick pan from beneath the counter then placed it on the stove. While she waited for it to get hot, she strolled over by the dinette table and glanced out the window. The morning sun now shone brightly over the backyard and glistened down on the river. Willa's next-door neighbor, Fred, walked along the wooden dock, taking in the morning. A minute later, he entered his boat parked on the other side across from Drake's yacht.

What is Braylon doing? Remembering how close Braylon had stood to her earlier this morning, her body tingled. She made her way back over to the stove and poured one-fourth of the sweet-scented pancake mixture into the frying pan. The top of the batter bubbled quickly. Using a spatula, she flipped it over.

When she pivoted to turn on the laptop sitting on the counter behind her, she noticed a present wrapped in glittery silver paper and tied with a big pink bow. *I wonder who this is for?*

The tiny envelope beneath the bow had her name on it. *For me? Willa shouldn't have.* She hefted the pretty package to her ear and shook it. She then put a finger under the back of the envelope, slitting it open.

Clenching the card in her hands, she began to read.

My Dearest Sandella,

While looking through the albums in the library the other day, I came across some pictures of you and your family. Grandma and Adam told me that the photos were important to you, so I decided to make you a present. When I first laid eyes on you my heart smiled. I hope your heart is now smiling, too.

I'm glad we met,

Braylon

Sandella's heart swelled with joy. Anxious to see what was inside the square box, her fingers pulled loose the shimmery paper. She lifted the lid and set it aside. Inside the box was a small pink photo album.

She flipped open the first page. Her heart ticked softly as she marveled over the black and white photo of her grandmother. *I forgot Willa had this picture. Oh Braylon, this is too much,* she thought, flipping to the second page.

Her heart strummed like a violin when she laid eyes on the picture of her mother, the love of her father's life. Long black hair, medium brown eyes, Sandella knew she looked just like Sugar in this picture. A smile took over her lips as she turned to the last page to find a photo of herself standing by the river in Willa's backyard.

She held the lovely present tight up against her chest. Tears stained her eyes. He'd put a lot of thought into the gift and it was the most beautiful present anyone had ever given her, definitely the most thoughtful. *How do I ever—*

The smoke alarm blared. She spun around. Dropping the album, her heart dunked. *The pancakes are burning!* Smoke billowed from the pan on the stove, rapidly clogging the air.

She took off for the stove and collided with Braylon's solid chest. Stepping around her, he grabbed the pot and tossed it into the dishwater inside the sink. A big loud poof resounded in her ears.

With the alarm bleeping, piercing her eardrums, Braylon curled his big hands around her biceps. Tilting her head back, she saw concern fill his gaze. "Are you okay?"

The feel of his strong hands holding her aroused her in a way she'd never experienced before. "I'm fine." She coughed, wondering how long it'd take before he tried to get her into his bed.

Chapter Three

BRAYLON'S DICK HURT BAD WITH a capital B while standing behind Sandella inside the garage. He ordered his tingly member to remain soft inside his drawers. The last thing he needed was to embarrass himself by getting a fucking erection.

He pulled open the passenger's side door of his grandfather's yellow convertible Jaguar that he'd said he could borrow anytime he wanted. Braylon stepped to the side and, as she climbed in, he enjoyed the wonderful site of her plump firm butt. The black jeans she wore complimented her big bubble behind, and threatened to make the tip of his head milk. *I wouldn't mind caressing that ass of hers.*

After he got Royce settled in the back seat of the car, he slid between the seat and the wheel, and started backing out of the driveway.

"So where are we going?" Sandella asked.

"It's a surprise." Braylon hit a button near the dashboard prompting the top to slide backward. "I hope you like seafood."

"I LOVE SEAFOOD." SHE COULD just stare at his face all day, every day. As he drove the Jaguar along the coast, the warm autumn wind connected with her skin, pricked her scalp. "Royce loves seafood, too." She looked back over her shoulder at Royce. He stared back at her with a big smile on his face.

His eyes diverted from her to Braylon. "Br...Br...Bray," he tried.

She looked at Braylon, then back at Royce. "Braylon. He's your nephew."

He nodded. "Braylon," he said it correctly, then burst into laughter at his achievement.

Smiling, Sandella applauded. "Good job, Royce! Good job!"

Braylon's smooth lips spread across his handsome face. "I know the family has already said it a million times, I'm sure. But thanks for all the hard work you put in with him. The last time I saw him he wasn't talking at all."

"You don't have to thank me. I love what I do. Besides making my pies, this is the only job for me. Speaking of my pies, I have to be back by three to make my afternoon deliveries."

"Well, I guess we better not spend too much time eating because I was hoping to take a stroll on the beach after lunch."

"That'll be nice," she said, thinking her father would roll over and die if he knew about any of this.

Minutes later Braylon drove into the parking lot of the Chart House, situated on the ocean, and parked. "The food here is great."

"So I've heard, but I've never been."

During lunch Sandella had the pleasure to indulge in the flavorful Lowcountry perloo shrimp and grits dish. She'd even tried some of Braylon's fried chicken and jalapeno and cheese biscuit, which was delicious too. Judging by Royce's empty plate, she could only assume the shrimp fritters she'd ordered for him were to die for.

After lunch, the three of them walked side by side with her in the middle along the pristine sandy beach of the ocean. A light breeze rustled off the shore blowing strands of her hair across her lips. She swiped her hair behind her ears.

"Thanks for lunch." The corners of his mouth turned up into a sweet smile that melted her heart.

"Thanks for joining me," he said, taking her hand into his.

A hot zing of electricity zapped up her arm making her nipples curl tight. His hand, so big, so hard, had her sizzling inside. If the touch of his hand made her nipples erect, *my goodness*, what would his mouth make her feel if he tasted them?

The two of them had a wonderful time getting better acquainted. Belatedly they turned around and made their way back toward the restaurant. When they reached the dock of the Chart House, a gentleman burst from the side door of the restaurant and accidentally bumped into Sandella.

"I'm sor—" The black man's eyes stretched wide. Wearing a white apron, he was dressed like a cook. She recognized the man immediately. "Sandella, my gawd, I ain't seen you since the day of your mother's funeral," he drawled in a Gullah accent. Of all the people to run into, why did it have to be her father's good friend, Claude?

"It's been a long time, Claude." Her bottom lip trembled lightly as she fought the urge to run.

He reached into the pocket of his apron and slid his glasses up the bridge of his bony nose. Taking in her face, he squinted. "I tell you…you sure are pretty. You look just like your momma."

If she hadn't been so nervous, she probably would've blushed. "Thanks."

His eyes left her face to take in Braylon's instead. "Is this your boyfriend?" he asked, checking him out from head to toe.

"Yes," Braylon blurted, untruthfully.

Sandella's jaw dropped. On the verge of going on a destructive rampage over the lie he'd told, she pinched her lips tight to keep from yelling. If Claude ran back and told her father she had a boyfriend and he was a Marine, Kane would have a meltdown. And there was no telling what he'd do.

He stuck out his hand and Claude shook it. "I'm Braylon Wexler."

With a fist on his hip, Claude tilted his head back as if he were thinking. "Wexler. Wexler." He snapped his fingers. "You kin to Willa and Drake?"

Braylon smiled. "Yes, sir. I'm their grandson."

"You that Marine Willa's been bragging to everybody about. I tell you fella, you got you a mighty fine gal, here. They don't make them like Sandella no more. Well, I got to get back to work before they fire me. Tell Kane I said hello and I'mma try to make my way to Beaufort to see him one day real soon."

Sandella's fingers fanned the air waving goodbye. "Okay. I will."

"Y'all two take care now. And don't let nobody get in the way of what you got." He reached in his pocket, took out a pack of cigarettes, and headed down toward the ocean.

"I can't believe you!" Sandella snapped.

"You're not mad about the boyfriend thing are you?" He laughed as if his lie was funny.

She grabbed Royce's hand. "You're darn right I am," she spat, hurrying for the car, walking vigorously in front of him. *Please don't let Claude tell Dad he saw me with my supposed Marine boyfriend.*

BY THE TIME THEY DROVE up to the estate Sandella had cooled

off. It'd been mighty cocky of Braylon to tell Claude he was her lover. By the same token, once he'd apologized, she'd found his outburst of a joke sort of charming. Besides, if her intuition was correct, any woman would be lucky to have a man like him to call her own.

Sandella stood at the bottom of the staircase watching Royce ascend the steps toward his bedroom so he could go take a nap. The entire way home from the restaurant he'd mentioned how sleepy he was. Once he reached the top and rounded the corner into his room, she sauntered inside the kitchen.

Braylon was standing by the counter where her caramel pecan pies were. "I'm ready for that dessert you promised." He lifted the caramel pecan pie she'd made earlier that morning right after the fire and sniffed it. "It sure smells good. How about we have dessert outside under the tree?"

How romantic. I'd love to. She gestured toward the door. "Lead the way."

Once outside under the tree, she sat on the ground next to him. She carved out a slice of pie, placed it on a round ceramic dish, and handed it to him. She then cut a piece for herself.

Braylon halved the pie with his fork and tasted it. "Mmm, mmm, mmm. This is delicious, Sandella."

She flushed. "Thank you."

"The best I've ever had. Have you thought about selling your pies in a store?"

"No."

"Well you should."

"Thanks."

"You have such a nice smile. I like you better when you're not mad at me."

"If you hadn't done what you did, then I would've never gotten mad at you. That was pretty cocky, you know?"

"I don't call it cocky."

She tilted her head. "Well, what do you call it?"

"Confident. You have some pie in the corner of your mouth. Is it okay if I get it off?"

"Yes, please do." She leaned her head forward thinking he would wipe the dessert off with his finger. Instead, he slanted his mouth over hers and kissed her. Cupping her shoulders, he slipped his tongue deeper into her mouth, and a husky groan escaped her. The sweet caramel flavoring of her pie rolled off his probing flesh and into her mouth where she gladly tasted it.

As he feasted hard on her mouth she felt like she was floating. Moist heat gathered in her core. *At last, at last. He's kissing me at last.*

He broke their heated kiss, leaving her mouth scorching like a raging wildfire. He swiped a piece of hair behind her ear, and breathed huskily against her swollen lips. "That was beautiful."

A hard pulse beat at the base of her throat as she sought to regulate her erratic breathing. His tender ministrations had her eyes misting. "Yes, it was."

BRAYLON WITNESSED WATER PUDDLE THE rims of Sandella's eyes. *Damn!* He hoped he wasn't moving too fast. *But damn*, he couldn't help it. This woman had his balls knotting and wanting to unload.

"What's wrong?"

"Nothing."

"They why are your eyes watery?"

She touched her swollen lips. "Braylon ...your kiss...made me feel something I've never felt before."

"Something good or bad?"

In a soft voice, she answered, "Good."

He brushed her cheek with the pad of his thumb. "I enjoyed our kiss, too. Let me taste you," he pecked her lips, "again." He pressed his open lips to hers, and swerved his tongue inside her mouth. His cock sang with electricity, then hardened like steel. *I can't wait to make love to you, my pretty lady.*

Tempted to roam his hand over her rounded breasts, he ran his fingers through her soft hair. He'd enjoyed licking the salty remnants of caramel from her sweet tongue.

He was reluctant to pause, but had to in order to catch his breath. Her eyes glowed affectionately, turning his heart to mush. Sperm boiled in his hard spheres. Aroused to the point of exploding, he put the tip of his nose on hers. "Sandella, I'm going to show you," he kissed her lips, "and prove to you," another kiss on her wet lips, "that I'm worthy of you." He sealed his promise with a final kiss.

Suddenly, his ex, Madison, and her son Drayton coursed through his mind. *Damn. Is Drayton my son?* Knowing he possibly had a young precious son, his heart wrenched.

Would Sandella have let him kiss her if she knew he might have a child? If Drayton turned out to be his, then he'd have no choice but to end things with Sandella. She deserved a man who could give himself completely and wholeheartedly. And the last thing he wanted was to end up the kind of man his father had been.

Wayne Wexler had been a no-good son of a bitch. After twenty-five years of marriage, Wayne had left his mother, Lorna, for his younger mistress. At the time of his parents' divorce, Braylon was in high school, and he'd promised himself then that he'd never walk out on his children and not raise them. *Never.*

His cell vibrated against his hip. He pulled it from the clip and read the screen. *Hell!* It was Madison. Talk about coincidence. Because he needed privacy when speaking with her, he slid the phone back into the clip and let the call roll to voicemail.

Sandella's gaze clung to the river. She bent her legs then wrapped her arms around them. She seemed like she was as deep in thought as he'd been seconds ago.

"What are you thinking about?" he prompted.

"Nothing."

"Sandella," he rubbed circles on her back, "I read people very well and I can tell you're thinking about something. I want you to share your feelings and thoughts with me. Look...to break the ice, why don't you tell me about those beautiful women in the photo album. And I'll tell you about myself and my family. Deal?"

She nodded. "Deal."

Braylon positioned his back up against the thick bark. He patted the space on the ground between his thighs. "Sit here." She crawled over him and sat between his thighs. Good thing his erection had softened.

Resting his chin on her shoulder, he eased his arms around her tiny waist, peered out at the river. *Man oh man, having her on me like this feels like heaven.* His cock throbbed. *Stay down, boy.*

Reddish orange leaves spiraled gracefully from the limbs sprinkling down over them. The warm autumn day and setting were perfect for kissing, sharing, and making love. *Don't try to bed her too soon*, he warned himself, inhaling her sweet, flowery scent.

"I haven't talked about my mother with anyone other than my family since the day she died."

He cupped her hands. "There's a first time for everything. I've been told I'm a good listener."

A heavy sigh pressed from her opened mouth. "She was such a beautiful woman, both inside and out."

He put his mouth to her lobe. "Yes, she was beautiful. You look just like her in the photo."

"She loved me and my brothers and my father so much. We were her world." Sandella's body relaxed within his strong embrace as she told him all about her grandmother's upbringing, and how she'd picked cotton in the fields of South Carolina for a living.

After reliving the happy life she'd had as a young teenager, she then moved on to the disastrous day her mother had died. He hadn't expected her to tell him at this particular moment. As she opened her mouth to speak, her body tensed. "It was raining hard the night she died," her voice cracked.

RAIN POUNDED THE SLICK ASPHALT as Sandella drove down the dark narrow road toward her home in Beaufort. Large balls of hail dropped from the sky, cracking against the windshield. Pressing her breastbone to the steering wheel in an attempt to see better, she flicked her windshield wipers to full speed.

Thunder boomed! She flinched. God, she hated driving in bad weather.

When she reached the cul-de-sac near her home, she noticed an army of police cars swarming her house. Even in the thickness of the heavy rainfall, red and blue flashing lights emanating from police cars blazed straight through the darkness.

With her heart drumming in her chest, Sandella hopped out of the car and bolted up the driveway. An officer standing at the foot of the porch steps stopped her from going inside the house. After showing him her driver's license verifying she lived there, the officer let her in.

She rushed passed her brother Drew weeping pitifully in the corner, and shot straight inside her parents' bedroom. Her heart shattered like broken glass. Her mother's mangled body lay on the stretcher with her father by her side.

She stood on the other side of the stretcher staring into her mother's pale face. Her eyes were closed and she looked dead. Panic rose inside her.

"What happened?" she asked, shaken, her eyes combing over the red bruises staining her mother's face, throat, and arms.

Her father's grim voice cracked as he said, "Someone broke into the house—"

The paramedic burst in. "She was raped and stabbed. We have get her to the hospital now."

"Waaiitt," her mother slowly breathed out, opening her eyes. "Saannddy." She grunted in pain as she flexed her fingers signaling for Sandella's hand. "Promise me."

"Promise you what?" Sandella asked, brushing errant bangs from her mother's forehead.

"Prrromiise." The whispered word slurred from her mother's swollen lips. "Take care of your brothers."

"You're going to be fine. I don't need to promise."

Her mother swallowed, closed her eyes, then reopened them. "Promise," she whispered. Blood was caked in the cracks of her inflamed, now purpling lips.

"Yes, Momma. I promise I'll take care of them." The depths of Sugar's eyes revealed deep love for her only daughter. Sandella pecked her mother's cold cheek.

She wheezed. "I think I'm dying." With her lips quivering, she half smiled.

Sandella started sobbing. "Please don't leave me, Momma."

"I taught you everything you need to know," she said, "so you could fly on your own. Now fly." Her eyes rolled closed.

"And that's what happened," Sandella said, blowing Braylon's mind. "A private told my father he'd heard it'd been another Marine who'd killed her. But he wouldn't say who. The police never bothered to question the man either."

"Why not?"

"According to them, there wasn't probable cause. A month late the private was found murdered in the woods."

"He was on to something."

"That's how my family and I felt."

"I'm so, so, sorry, Sandella," he said, squeezing her.

Her shoulders sagged. "I just feel if the killer was brought to justice, my father would finally be able to relax. He worries so much about me."

His stomach roiled in disgust. *If someone hurt her, I'll kill the bastard.* A strong need to protect her surfaced inside him. "Tell your father that he doesn't have to worry about you now that I'm here."

"That's nice of you to say."

"I didn't say it to be nice. I said it because I meant it." Braylon didn't understand the newfound gentleness tugging at his heart for the damn woman.

"Do you know if there's any way I can go about reopening the case?"

You're damn right there is. "There's a loophole in everything. I'll see what I can do." *My eyes and ears are going to be wide open when I start work on this criminal investigation.*

"I'd appreciate anything you can do."

"Don't mention it. It's my job." Snuggling his cheek against the softness of her unruly hair, he kissed her tresses. *I'm going to find out who killed your mother, baby. I damn sure am.*

Chapter Four

SANDELLA'S HANDS CURLED AROUND THE steering wheel as she made her way across town toward her home in Beaufort. She glanced over at Royce, then returned her focus to the street. She lowered the visor to protect her vision from the orange glowing sun surrounded by hues of coral blues. She could imagine herself and Braylon walking along the coast with that same sun as the backdrop. *He's such a great kisser. He makes me so hot.*

Still reeling over the way Braylon had left her mouth scorching from their sizzling kiss, her nipples tingled. The lusty fantasy of his tongue leaving her mouth to lick her breasts aroused her. What a shame it was to have such sexual desires for a man who hadn't even kissed her there yet.

Yet? Would Braylon would be her first lover? The man she lost her virginity to? The man that could put her father in an early grave if he found out about them? She shook her head to shake off the notion. *I can't let that happen. I just can't. But how do I control what I'm feeling? How do I deny myself him if he tries to seduce me?*

Fifteen minutes after crossing the bridge, Sandella steered her car into the driveway of her home and parked. "Let's go, Royce." She grabbed her purse, they both exited, and they started up the driveway.

As she clambered the steps to the porch, her father's angry voice stabbed the cool evening air. *What in the world is going on?* She opened the creaking screen door and stepped inside. Royce tagged along behind her.

"I said get in your room! Now!" Kane's deep voice throttled angrily. Apparently her father was having an altercation with Drew. But what in the world for? Drew was such a good kid. "Right now!"

Royce jumped. He grabbed Sandella's hand and squeezed it so hard she thought he'd crack the bones. The shouts had him trembling.

Sandella let go of Royce's hand and clamped his shoulders. "It's okay, Royce. Please don't be scared," she said, her hands running up and down his arms.

Royce nodded in understanding. "Okay."

The floorboards creaked, alerting her that her father was heading in her direction. Wondering what in the heck was going on she turned to face the narrow hallway. Kane's hands clenched the wheels of the chair as he steered himself inside the living room.

Her father's bottom lip rolled under. "That brother of yours has lost his damn mind! He's grounded for a whole month!"

A month? She put her hands on her hips and spoke softly. "Dad, could you please lower your voice? Royce is terrified of yelling."

Kane's bitter voice came out low as he spoke through clenched teeth. "Your brother can't be trusted."

Drew isn't disrespectful. This has to be a misunderstanding. Sandella tilted her head. "What did he do, Dad?"

Kane drew a cigarette from his shirt pocket and waved it at Sandella. "Nettie Mae called me. She told me that one of her cackling-mouth friends saw Drew over at Colonel Barton's house playing football in the goddamn backyard. I have told him over and over not to go inside any of those Marines' houses."

Hearing the malice for Marines in her father's voice sickened her. Sighing, her breath came out harsh. She rubbed her temples hoping she'd soothe away the dull pain in her head. *I was with a Marine earlier today too,* was on the brink of spilling from her lips.

Braylon and I don't stand a freaking chance. "Dad, don't you think you're being a little hard on him?"

He held the lighter to the end of the cigarette. His brows gathered in the center of his forehead. His cheeks sucked inward as he inhaled and smoke spiraled from his brown lips. The cold stare in his round black eyes chilled her. "Your mother was killed by a Marine. For all I know Barton may be the damn killer," he said, lowering the cigarette to the ashtray on the table by the wall.

He has to stop with all this. "The Bartons seem like such a good family. From what I hear their sons are straight-A students like Drew. It's not good to shelter him, Dad. Isn't it better for him to be around teenagers that are doing well, than to hang out with—"

"I'm not changing my mind, Sandy. Now follow me." Kane steered the chair around and rolled himself down the hallway.

What if Claude calls and tells him he saw me with Braylon at the restaurant on the beach? Dear God, please let this stay our little secret. With Royce behind her, she followed her father into the master bedroom. A chill enveloped her. God, she'd never get used to going inside this room, the room where her mother was raped and murdered.

Although they'd changed the furniture around, replaced the bedspread, and painted the walls a bright ivory color, she still could see the bloody images of her mother's dying body as if she'd been killed just yesterday. Maybe if they got another house her father would be able to see things differently, be able to finally heal and move on with his life. Maybe she would be able, too. Who was she kidding? They couldn't afford another house.

Kane hunched over in his chair and pulled open the drawer to the nightstand. He hefted a brown wooden case then turned to face her. "After Nettie Mae told me about Drew, I went out and bought you something."

"What?" she asked.

"Close the door," Kane ordered.

Her eyes turned to Royce. "Is it okay if Royce stays in here with us? If not, I can have him wait in the living room."

Kane shook his head. "I don't mind him hearing what I have to say. He doesn't talk so I don't have to worry about him repeating it."

"He is talking now. And he understands more than you think he does. He's even reading."

"That's good he's reading. I'm proud of you, Sandy. Let him stay."

Kane's eyes narrowed as he looked at Royce. "Everything that goes on in this room remains quiet. You hear me?"

Royce didn't answer. He just stared at Kane.

"Damn, Sandy. I thought you said this here boy could talk."

"He does. He just doesn't talk much. I'm still working on his communication skills."

"Now that doesn't make any sense to me. He can read, but he doesn't talk. Sounds damn near crazy."

She sighed. "Dad, please." As much as she loved her father he was starting to get on her last nerve. As soon as she fixed dinner for him and Drew she was heading back to the estate. She might even take Drew with her if Kane agreed.

"Look here, Royce," Kane said. "You protect my daughter if one of those damn Marines comes near her, you hear?"

Her headache had filled her entire forehead by this point.

Silence.

Kane cleared his throat. "Anyway. As I was saying...I bought this for you." With the case sitting in his lap, he pulled back the lid.

Her heart squeezed. Inside the compartment lay a shiny black pistol. She placed a hand to her chest.

"My God, Dad. A gun? Really? A gun!"

Royce patted the top of his head repetitively while gritting his teeth. He did this often whenever he became nervous.

"You better calm down, Sandy. Your friend there is getting nervous."

Sandella rubbed gentle circles on Royce's back. "It's okay, Royce. I'm sorry for yelling." She smiled. He lowered his hand to his side, and smiled back.

Kane's gaze shifted to the pistol then back up to her face. He extended the case to her. "I bought this here beauty for you. If Colonel Barton or any of those Marines come near you, I want you to blow their fucking heads off. Don't even hesitate. Just shoot the shit out of them." *Dear Lord.* "Starting tomorrow, I'm going to teach Drew how to shoot, too."

Feeling overwhelmed, she folded her arms beneath her breasts. "Don't you think you're overreacting? I mean...not all Marines are bad. I'm sure there're more good ones than bad ones." *Especially the one that nearly sucked my face off earlier...I loved every minute of it, too.*

His eyes widened. After putting the case on the bed, he wheeled himself as close as possible to her, leaving hardly any space. He glared. "The day," he bared his teeth, "you let your guard down and began to trust one of those Marines..." He swallowed, his Adam's apple gliding up and down. "...is the day you're going to end up just...like...your...mother," he clipped out.

The dark malice swirling inside his pupils caused her own eyes to mist. Kane's tremendous grief pained her. Standing before him, she mentally prayed that God someday, real soon, would heal his broken heart. She'd give anything for him to be whole and happy again. "I love you, Daddy."

Bobbing his head, he sniffed. "I love you too, baby girl." A tear slipped from his eye and ran down over his coarse beard. "I ain't taking any chances of losing you or your brother, like I lost your mother. I'll kill anybody that tried to hurt any of my children." He handed her the case with the loaded gun.

First thing tomorrow morning she would end her budding relationship with Braylon. Of course she'd still be cordial to him. But she wasn't going out with him anymore.

Why me? If her father hadn't been sitting there, she'd slap the hell out of her forehead.

"Another thing. After Drew graduates, I'm selling the house and moving to an apartment."

"You're what? What about me?" she asked, though she knew she could take care of herself.

"I know you're taking college courses online, but I want you to finish your last year on an actual campus, like you'd been planning to do before your mother died. I don't have much money, but the little I do have, and whatever I get from the house, will be yours."

Sniffing, she pressed her hands together in a prayer symbol over her mouth. "Dad, I can't take money from you. You may need it someday."

Kane rolled his eyes. "You *will* take the money and go to college. It's an order, not a question, Sandy."

After she got her business degree, maybe she could go to culinary school and become one of the world's greatest chefs. Perhaps her caramel pecan pies would become a hit like Braylon had said they would. Although she had no intentions of taking money from him, she wrapped her arms around her father and squeezed him tightly.

"The Wexlers had an emergency and had to leave town. After I talk with Drew and make dinner, Royce and I will be heading back to the estate."

"Whew! Thank God y'all ain't staying here. The last time they went out of town and he stayed here, he was up all night scraping his nails against the walls. I didn't get any sleep." With an elbow on the arm of the chair, he touched his forehead. "He scared me half to death."

"Do you have to be so animated all the time?"

Kane's brows arched. "Me. Animated? I thought that there boy was going to whoop my ass that night."

"Ass. Ass," Royce mocked Kane.

"Well, I'll be damn. He can talk. He likes curse words, I see."

She smiled. "You're too much, Dad." A light chuckle escaped her as she turned and headed out the door.

"Good seeing you, Royce. And thanks for taking care of my daughter," Kane said, after them. "And don't worry about cooking, Sandy. Drew and I can eat a frozen dinner or something."

When Sandella entered Drew's room, she found him sitting on the bed propped up with a pillow. He looked as gloomy as ever. "Hey, Drew. How's it going?" She sat on the mattress next to him.

He sucked his teeth. "It's not going. I'm tired of Dad being mean and judging people because of their jobs. We are surrounded by military families. He put me on punishment for going over to Troy's house. Troy is a great dude. There's nothing wrong with him. Or his brother. Or his father and mother."

"Me either. Just so you know, I disagree with Dad."

"I can't wait to get out of this house. One more year, and I'm getting as far away from Beaufort as I possibly can. Just like Aric and Chandler went to college, I'm going, too. And like them, I'm never coming back."

She nodded.

"I'm glad you see things my way," Drew said.

"Dad is still grieving Mom. Don't be too hard on him."

"We all are still hurting over Momma. But we have to go on. We can't stop living our lives. She wouldn't want us to do that. Not even Dad."

"You're right, Drew. You're absolutely right."

Drew sucked his teeth. "Momma raised us to love all people, not to be prejudiced. Men and women are in Iraq protecting our country and Dad has the nerve to be judging them."

Sandella said, "I think he's depressed. I'm going to see about getting him some counseling."

Drew burst out into laughter. "If you think his stubborn behind is going to get some counseling, then you're more naïve than I thought."

Sandella joined him in his bout of giggles. "You're right. Dad is stuck in his ways. It'd be a cold day—"

"In hell before he goes to see a psychiatrist." Drew threw his hands up in the air. "Staying in the house for a whole month is going to drive me up the wall."

Apprehensive about the sudden decision to alter her father's ruling, she nibbled on her bottom lip. "I have an idea."

"What?"

"I'm going to convince Dad that it'll be better for you to volunteer at the community center than to sit home and play the PlayStation when he's not watching. That way, you can still be around your friends after school."

Drew's face lit up with a smile. He snatched the controller from the dresser, and clicked on the television. "And play basketball, and pool, and lift weights. Thank God you're here to look out for me. I hope you don't leave until after I'm gone." His fingers shifted the control keys on the PlayStation's control.

"Aw, don't mention it."

"Dinner will be ready in about thirty minutes."

For dinner Sandella cooked a good southern meal consisting of Cajun butterflied fried shrimp, fried catfish, and a big bowl of spicy southern potato salad. After washing the dishes, she helped Drew with his homework, then she and Royce headed back to Hilton Head Island.

Driving along the road in the thick of the night she shifted in her seat. For some reason she felt she was coming down with something. Perhaps she had a virus, or was getting the flu. Her head ached, and her body felt warmer than normal. Maybe she wasn't sick at all. Maybe her dad's negative attitude toward Marines had her more upset than she cared to admit. She turned the air conditioner to full blast in an effort to cool off.

Glints of the full bright moon cast a sensual glow through the windshield. Before speaking with her father this evening, she probably would've been able to imagine herself and Braylon sitting in the backyard at the estate under the tree, sharing another passionate kiss, and eventually making love. But now the only thing she could imagine was Braylon running away from her father with a gun pointing at his back.

I'll have to apologize to Braylon for misleading him.

AFTER GETTING ROYCE TO BED, Sandella stood at the window in the guest bedroom on the second level of the mansion. She drew back the red velvet curtains and peered down at the cottage. A single light gleamed brightly inside the bedroom. *He's finally home.*

A few minutes later she stood at the cottage's door going over the script she'd rehearsed inside her head. *While I enjoyed our kiss, I'm sorry for misleading you. Because I know it'll lead to nothing but trouble, it can't happen again.* Of course, her practiced speech sounded downright stupid, but she had no choice but to let him know that they couldn't engage in anything of the sort ever again.

Just as she raised her hand to knock on the door it peeled open. The foyer's bright light shined down on Braylon and he looked like a handsome, fine warrior. Admiring the tight grey fabric spreading across his brawny chest, she felt the color drain from her face. She mentally slapped the hell out of her forehead a dozen times as air clogged her throat.

"I was just coming to see you." His deep voice sent chills up her spine.

Lordy Jesus. He's hot. "You were? Why?"

"I wanted to know if you'd like to watch a movie on demand with me. I heard *White House Down* was pretty good."

"We need to talk." She walked straight past him into the living room. As he closed the door a cinnamon fragrance streamed up her nose. *I wonder what it'd be like to smooth cinnamon icing over his chest and lick it off his nipples? Or better yet, his penis. A cinnamon penis? Mmmm.* Her tongue involuntarily darted out of her mouth, wetting her lips.

He towered over her. "So what do you want to talk to me about?"

Okay, what I have to say will sound stupid, but I can do this.

She cleared her throat. "After much thought I—"

"Please sit down." He gestured toward one sofa then flopped down on the one opposite it.

Sandella took a seat across from him then crossed her legs at the knees. As she sought the words to end their romantic friendship, she took in the masculinity of his olive-skinned face.

Gliding his arms along the curve of the sofa, he spread his legs wide open. A huge knot pressed against the fabric of his cotton black shorts, sending the inside of her mouth to salivating. *Oh, my now. Look-a-there. Look-a-there.*

"Sandella."

She snapped her eyes up to look at his face once more. *That thing looked huge!*

"What were you saying?"

Her head spun with confusion. She'd never come close to wanting a man like this before. She steepled her fingers in her lap. "I've been thinking and..."

Nausea rose in her stomach. *My dad doesn't want me seeing you. How childish does that sound?*

Now that she was sitting here in front of him, she knew if she told him that she didn't want to see him again, or kiss him again, or touch him again...it'd all be one big lie. Right now, more than anything, she wanted him to hold her, and tell her everything would be okay, and they'd live happily ever after. She'd really lost it now.

"You been thinking and..." Braylon came and sat beside her. "Are you okay?"

She still felt sick from earlier today. She placed a hand to her belly. "I feel queasy," she said, being completely truthful. Bile scratched the back of her throat. She felt as if her body had gotten hotter since she'd returned back to the estate.

"You don't look so good."

"I feel like I have to—" She slapped a hand over her mouth, and took off for the bathroom. Halfway there, she vomited on the carpet. Knowing another round of foul bile was about to escape her, she staggered inside the bathroom and purged inside the toilet.

After flushing, she looked back over her shoulder at Braylon. A concerned look softened his features. "What can I do to help you?"

"I need to lie down," she said, standing and feeling faint. Her head spun as a slow wave of heat spread through her bones.

"Let me help you to the bed." He yanked her off her feet and carried her to the bedroom. He turned back the cover and lowered her to the mattress.

He put the back of his hand to her forehead. "You feel

extremely hot," he said, smoothing her bangs in with the rest of her hair on top of her head. "Where's the thermometer?"

Why was she so exhausted? she wondered, taking in the worried expression shadowing his face. "There's one in the kitchen cabinet next to the refrigerator inside the main house."

"I'll be right back." Braylon dashed out the front door to the main house, and quickly returned. "Let me take your temperature."

Sweat beaded on her forehead. When she tried to sit up, her attempt failed. "I felt bad earlier when I was visiting my dad, but now I feel awful."

Braylon swept the hair covering the side of her face behind her ear and took her temperature. He dropped his face closer to hers. With his fingers to her chin, he turned her face away from his toward the pleated sheers. "One hundred and three degrees. And your neck is covered with red spots."

"It is?"

He grabbed the mirror off the dresser and handed it to her. "Take a look."

Sandella peeked into the mirror. A bumpy red rash covered the sides and back of her neck. To her knowledge she wasn't allergic to anything. *I must've eaten something bad.* "I have no clue what this is." Mustering what little strength she had, she shifted sideways and put her feet to the floor.

"You're in no shape to get out of bed."

"I need to take a look at the rest of my body."

Braylon's eyes glittered with amusement. "I can take a look for you if you like."

Even in her ill state she managed a curt smile. "No, thank you. I'll do it myself."

Holding her hand, he guided her to the bathroom. She placed a hand on the door frame. "No visitors allowed," she said, shutting the door in his face.

Standing in front of the mirror, Sandella gathered her shirt at the hem and removed it. She turned to look at her back. She gasped. Blisters were gathered on her back like a bad case of red leaking acne. "Oh my God!"

The door flung open. "What!" He gawked at her practically nude chest.

Her hands shot up to her breasts in an attempt to cover them and the black satin bra she was wearing. She felt blood gather in her cheeks. "Braylon! You can't come in here!"

"I'm sorry. But you scared me half to death when you screamed." Starting with her hair, his eyes rolled up and down her body. "God, you're so beautiful," he said, entering the bathroom. His eyes left her face and traveled to the mirror. "What in the world is that on your back?"

She shrugged. "I don't know if it's my imagination or what, but it's starting to itch really, really, bad."

"I'm taking you to the doctor." He grabbed her shirt off the counter and redressed her.

"I can drive myself to the hospital. Why don't you stay here with Royce? I just hate waking him."

"That's nonsense. I'm taking you, period…end of subject." He tugged her hand, guided her outside to the yellow convertible he'd grown accustomed too over the past few weeks.

Sandella watched Braylon enter the house through the back door of the garage. The affectionate way he was taking care of her stirred a tender emotion. *Not all Marines are bad, Dad. Especially not my Braylon.*

Chapter Five

AFTER LEAVING THE HOSPITAL, BRAYLON drove to the other side of the island to drop Royce off at his Aunt Gladys's home. Clutching the hospital blanket up to her chin, Sandella sat in the passenger's seat staring out the window, then transferred her gaze toward him. "I feel bad about Gladys having to care for Royce until I get better."

"Don't," he said, reaching over brushing the top of her head. "Willa doesn't want you taking care of him while you're recovering from a food intolerance. She wants you to get some rest and take care of yourself so you can get better. Grandma loves you like a daughter, you know?"

She nodded. "Yes, I know." *Is it possible that I'm allergic to peanut butter?*

It was shortly after midnight when Braylon steered the Jaguar up the circular driveway of the estate and parked. He rounded the car, opened the door, and hefted Sandella in his arms.

"Where are you taking me?" He carried her toward the guest cottage.

"You're staying with me tonight."

"But I have a room inside the main house," she said, looking at the dark mansion then back at his handsome face.

"You're sick and you're staying with me, and that's the end of the story." His tone was so sharp she didn't dare argue with him.

Too weak and exhausted to care anyway, she cuddled her head up against his thick chest as he carried her inside. He raised his leg and kicked the door closed.

"Please take me to the guest room."

He paused in his tracks, kissed her forehead. "I was hoping you'd sleep with me in my bed." His tone was deliberately charming, tempting her to give in. God, she'd love to lie next to him and let him hold her at a time like this. Certainly his strong biceps wrapped around her would feel like good medicine. But sleeping in his bed was too darn risky. There was no telling what she'd do if she did, no matter how sick she was.

The medicine the doctor had given her had made her feel much better, but not enough that she couldn't see that sleeping in his bed would do more harm than good. "I'll be sleeping in the guest room."

"Have it your way," he said, pivoting in the opposite direction.

As Sandella sat on the bed watching Braylon leave the guest room, she wanted to reach out and grab his elbow to stop him.

"Good night," she said.

"Good night, Sandella." The way he said her name put her heart in a tizzy. He closed the door, leaving her feeling wistful.

Deep down inside she wanted him in her bed just as much as he wanted her in his. Not so she could have sex with him, but just so he could hold her until the morning came.

After she showered, she strolled back inside the room to find one of Braylon's dress shirts on the bed. He must've come in and left it there while she was bathing. She shrugged her arms through the sleeves of the white cotton material to find his winter-fresh scent embedded in the fibers.

Wearing Braylon's shirt made her oddly happy. She pulled the beaded string on the lamp to turn off the light. She pulled the comforter up to her chin. As Sandella drifted off to sleep she had only one person on her mind—*my Braylon.*

The wind whistled ruefully. Sandella bolted upright in bed. A bolt of lightning coursed through the slits in the blinds, flashing inside the dark room. She flinched. Raindrops clanked against the rooftop, sounding like banging tin cans.

She hated that her father and Drew had gone on a fishing trip. Suddenly, the creaking sound of her back door opening terrified her. The hair on her neck stood on end. jumped out of bed and dropped to her knees.

Her hands fumbled beneath the bed for the box with the loaded weapon that her father had given her. She snatched the wooden case from beneath her bed then flipped the lid open.

A more intense strike of lighting cracked the sky, flashing down on the black pistol. She hefted the loaded gun into her quivering hands. She staggered to her feet.

Her heart plummeted at the sight of the tall shadowy figure emerging in the doorway. The man raised a shiny blade over his shoulder. "I killed your mother, now I'm going to kill you." The striking lighting bounced off the tip of the knife as he came toward her.

The gun shook in her trembling grip. She aimed at his chest. The killer halted. His wicked eyes narrowed. "You wouldn't."

Releasing a guttural groan, she fired a bullet straight into his heart.

"NOOO!"

Sandella's frantic screams jolted Braylon from his dream about flicking his tongue over her tight, erect bud. At first, he'd thought she'd been screaming while exploding inside his mouth. But when he heard her cries a second time, his heart tanked.

He snatched the covers from his bare torso and hopped out of bed. With his dick hard as a thick pipe against his abdomen he raced across the living room into the guest suite.

Sandella writhed and twisted beneath the covers as if she was fighting. He shook her. "Sandella! Wake up!"

Her eyes shot open. Her chest heaved up and down with each rapid breath. She sat upright and touched a hand to her forehead. "Oh God. I had a nightmare. It seemed so real."

He caressed her shoulder. "It's okay. I'm here, baby." he said, pulling the beaded string on the lamp. The dim light vaguely lit the room.

As her breathing returned to normal, Sandella cupped her neck. "My throat is dry."

"I'll be right back with some water."

Seconds later when Braylon returned she was still sitting up in bed with a bleak expression, staring at the wall. "I killed him," she said, turning her gaze toward him.

Braylon handed her the bottled water. "Who?"

"My mother's killer." She twisted the top off, tilted it to her mouth, and sipped. She let out a sorrowful sigh.

He gathered her in his arms and squeezed her tight. "You're safe with me, Sandella." He kissed the top of her head.

Her eyes misted. "I'm scared. Will you sleep in here with me tonight?" Long lashes shadowed her face.

"Of course I will." Braylon turned off the light and slipped beneath the covers beside her.

The moonlight sloped from the window, casting a glow over

their bodies. When she eased her back up against his chest, her butt scraped his flaccid penis. He swallowed hard. If she wriggled her ass up against him again, he wasn't going to take the blame for his rod turning to stone.

"Hold me, Braylon." Her genuine need slipped from her mouth in a soft sweet voice.

"Come here, baby." He wrapped her in his arms. Damn. Her tight ass cheeks stayed nestled against his penis. Now, did she really expect him to lie here next to her and not touch her? While she wiggled up against his dick…wearing nothing but a pair of panties and his dress shirt?

I want you bad, Sandella. Braylon stroked her arms. "Has the rash been bothering you?"

"Not since I took the medicine."

"Good. Let me know if you need anything." *By the way, do you need any dick?* he wanted to ask, but knew that the direct approach wouldn't be best. She was inexperienced. His fingers lingered on her collarbone.

Loving the way the soft curves of her backside fit into the hard lines of his torso sent his heart to thudding. Heat spooled in his hardening sac. She brought his hand to her lips and kissed it. Desire zapped straight to his loins. Damn!

Was she trying to let him know that it was okay if he made a move on her? No, she was too sick. Then again, she did say she felt better and that the medicine was working. *There's only one way to find out.* Wanting to make love to a woman while she was sick? He had a damn problem.

Aching to get inside her, he trailed his hand down her bare thigh. Her body tensed. "It's hard to lie here next to you and not touch you, Sandella."

Softly, she said, "I never said you couldn't touch me, Braylon." She rolled to her side and put a soft hand on his stubbly beard.

"Are you sure?" Nuzzling her nose, he pecked her soft lips. "I don't want you to do anything you don't want—"

Sandella's tongue darted from her lips straight into his mouth. His shaft knotted. Her smooth lips felt like cotton.

He groaned deep inside her throat as he kissed her. She pulled away, leaving his mouth aching to feast between her thighs. "I've wanted you from the very first day we met," he said. Her gaze was slumberous, sexy as hell. He raked his hands through her disorderly hair. "And I want you even more now." He nipped her bottom lip.

A sensual glow passed over her expressive brown face. "Me too." Her soft breath caressed the base of his neck urging him to recapture her swollen, wet lips.

As he slowly drank the feverish saliva from her mouth he cupped her breast and flicked a thumb over her erect nipple. She winced. The building magnetism between them was undeniable.

His fondling hand drifted from her breast to her flat belly then kneaded the tender flesh of her inner thigh. Pushing her panties to the side, he slipped a finger up in her wet core, curling a finger over her G-spot. She thrust her pelvis up against his stroking fingers and groaned huskily in his mouth.

Her hot sex drowned his fingers. *She's so fucking wet!* His balls tightened, his shaft throbbed. When he tugged then pressed the pad of his thumb to her beaded clitoris, she whimpered against his demanding lips. *Do I fuck her? Do I fuck her not?*

He trailed the tip of his tongue around the edges of her tender lips, then gently cupped her ear. "I want to eat you."

Excitement glowed in her irises. Her nodding signified her assent to have him lick her till she screamed his damn name. He mounted her, clenched her hips, then slid her petite body down the soft cotton sheets.

He rolled her panties down her slender legs, tossed them to the floor. About to burst, he spread her slick labia wide and positioned his nose to her black hard pearl. He inhaled her essence. The sweet scent of her drenched opening made the tip of his engorged head leak fluid. Dying to taste her pussy, he dropped his mouth on her and began lapping her inside out.

Her labia quivered against his mouth. *Best pussy in the world.*

Circling her hips, she clenched the sides of his head. "Oh, Braylon." Wanting to bring her sheer pleasure, he sucked hard on her clitoris while pumping her insides with two of his fingers.

She bucked like a fierce bull on his face as if she were about to explode. She reached down between her legs, cupped the back of his hand, and prompted him to thrash her harder.

With his head wobbling from side to side between her quaking legs, he reached up and flicked a finger over her nipple with one hand while still stroking her with the other. Her shaking thighs closed around his head, holding his face captive on her heated sex.

"Braylon!" His name tumbled from her lips. The hard beats of her canal pounded on his tongue as she climaxed inside his mouth. Coming up for air, he gladly drank the salty cream splattered on his lips.

His hard stem was stretched to the limit, squirming like a snake inside his drawers. *Damn, I'm hurting.* He got to his feet to pick her panties from the floor. Standing to the side of the bed, he guided her feet through the loops of her underwear then rolled the flimsy material up her legs, covering her.

"What's wrong?" she asked, bemused.

"Believe me, there's nothing wrong, Sandella."

She sat up and crossed her arms across her breasts. Disappointment spread across her face. "Then why aren't you trying to take things further? Don't you want to make love to me?"

He reached in his boxers, pulled out his hard dick, letting it pulsate in his fist. He looked down at his erection then back up at her face. "What does it look like to you?"

Her tongue rolled over her still enflamed lips. Her eyes widened. "It looks like you do."

He scooted next to her, palmed the back of her head, and nudged his forehead to hers. Before he knew it, she dropped her head into his lap, curled her hand around his shaft, and tried to wrap her lips around his thick head.

"God. No! Sandella! No!" He clenched the sides of her head and lifted her face from his erection. Gazing into her caramel, flickering eyes, he swallowed. "As much as I'd love for you to do that to me, tonight is not about me, baby," he said, his spheres heated into hot balls of fire. "It's about you, and only you."

"But—"

He shook his head defiantly. "But nothing, baby. Trust me," he put a finger to her chin, "what I have in store for you, you're going to need way more energy than what you have now." *I'd probably damn near kill her if I made love to her now.* "You need to rest first."

If she wasn't so sick, he'd flip her on her stomach and fuck her senseless. But the last thing he needed was for her to wake up sore, raw, and worst off than she already was with the damn rash. Besides the doctors had drugged her so much he wanted to make sure she was thinking with a clear head when he branded her with his lovemaking.

Swallowing, she nodded. "Okay."

"Now good night."

"Good night."

Lying back to back, Braylon's cock was so hard he could hardly see straight. At one point he contemplated rolling on his side to fuck her. Remembering how he'd curled his tongue over her hard clitoris, he finally fell sound asleep with his hand inside his pants, stroking his cock.

SANDELLA STIRRED. FEELING LIKE A train had derailed her body while stretched out on a track; she slowly peeled her eyes open to find the bright sun lighting up the white-walled room. She lay on her back looking up at the ceiling as a wave of nausea rolled in the pit of her stomach. The rash on her back itched and her head pounded. She felt like crap and needed her meds in a hurry.

Draping an arm over her forehead, memories of last night sailed inside her mind. Braylon had been right. It was a good thing she didn't have sex—well she did let him provide the best oral sex in the world to her. But as far as penetration, there was no way she could've handled that gigantic monster with the little strength she had.

The memory of being held against his rock hard body, licked by his long talented tongue, brought a smile to her face and a dull ache settled between her legs. Sick and craving him at the same time? Coming to understand that a woman's body could feel so many different emotions at one time had her bewildered. Then again, one look at the fine Braylon and she knew exactly why she needed his insatiable body on top of hers, making sweet tender love.

She sat upright, turned sideways on the bed, and plopped her feet up on the bed's wooden frame. With her elbow pressed into her thigh, she put her fist to her chin and glared across the room out the window at the river. *I've gotten myself into a mess. A mess I don't think I can get out of even if I wanted too. He has no clue I'm a virgin. Should I tell him?*

The bedroom door cracked wide open. Braylon emerged in the doorway smiling ever so handsome and lugging her soft pink suitcase behind him. "Good morning, beautiful," he said cheerily, coming to a stop in front of her.

She smiled. "Good morning." She tilted her head looking up at his gorgeous, masculine face. Her nipples rounded into hard black pebbles. *Here I go again.* Why couldn't she stop with all the tingling?

His potent woodsy fragrance assailed her nostrils. Overnight his dark beard had filled in on his gorgeous face. *Oh no...I think I'm in love.*

"Do you always wake up this pretty?" he asked huskily, smiling.

She blushed. "Thanks," she said, feeling she probably looked way worse than he was saying.

He plopped her suitcase up on the bed. "How did you sleep last night?"

After that good licking you gave me I slept just fine. "I slept well. What about you?"

"I slept off and on, had something heavy on my mind." He pushed the suitcase to the far end of the bed. When he sat on the mattress beside her, a subtle creak reverberated throughout the room.

As she yearned for him to hold her like he'd done last night, the skin of their arms touched. He grasped her hand. His darkening eyes worried her.

Please don't tell me you regret it. Bracing herself for the worse possible outcome, she swallowed, then shifted her gaze toward the wall. He clenched her chin and turned her face toward his, reconnecting their gazes. "What kept you up so much?" She could hear the worry in her own voice.

"Do you remember what happened last night?"

The way you made me orgasm in your mouth...how could I not? She nodded. "Yes. I remember everything."

"I'm sorry for taking advantage of you while you were sick, under strict doctor's orders and drugged out of your mind. I should've waited until you were able to think clearly before letting things go as far as they did. Please accept my apology." His thumb caressed the back of her hand.

Braylon's apology was so unnecessary. She'd known fully what she was engaging in, and had enjoyed every minute of the pleasurable acts. In fact, if she was feeling better at this moment she'd spread her legs and welcome him to explore her insides.

She placed her hand to the hard stubble of his jaw. "I knew exactly what I was doing, Braylon. If I had to do it all over again, I would," she said, becoming embarrassed after inhaling the familiar scent of her early morning breath. "I have no regrets."

His brows hitched. "Are you sure?"

"If anything, I owe you for taking me to the hospital, taking Royce to Gladys's, and helping me get to sleep after that horrible nightmare."

"I'm glad to hear that. The last thing I want you to feel is like I'm pressuring you to do something you're not interested in or ready for. Promise me that if I get ahead of myself, you'll let me know."

She raised her hand in a swearing position and smiled. "Scout's honor."

He chuckled while patting her thigh. "Good. The doctor said you may not have an appetite so I ran out to the store and bought you some fruit and bran muffins. They're on the counter in the kitchen."

She tilted her head. "Thanks. That was very sweet of you, but you shouldn't have troubled yourself."

"It was the least I could do and no trouble at all." He stood then tugged her hand. "Come with me. I have something I want you to do."

"Okay," she said, curious.

He led her across the living room into his bedroom then directly into the large powder-white bathroom. As her eyes roamed over the thoughtful romantic gesture he'd put together, butterflies twirled in the pit of her belly. *He did all of this while I was sleeping, dreaming of him.* With the tip of her index finger lingering on her bottom lip, she looked at him and smiled.

Water filled the oversized garden tub. Lavender rose petals floated along the surface. Music like the ocean's caress streamed from the speaker of his iPhone sitting on the marble counter. To top it off, her medication along with a bran muffin, fresh fruit, and a glass of orange juice sat on top of the vanity in front of the lighted oval mirror.

Impressed, she placed a hand over her heart. "My goodness. You thought of everything didn't you? Thank you so much."

"It's an oatmeal bath so it should help with the itching and rash."

"You are too much Mr. Wexler," she said, smiling. "Again... thank you."

"Ahhh, it's no big deal. I just want you to heal and get better." After lighting an orchid candle tucked in the corner of the tub, he left her standing in the center of the room simply amazed and appreciative. *I think he likes me. Really likes me.*

She brushed her teeth and gulped down the meds and bittersweet orange juice, then sunk her teeth into the delicious bran muffin. Braylon didn't miss a beat when planning her morning, she thought, tossing the muffin wrapper in the trash bin.

She turned up the blinds by the sink letting the morning sun stream inside. After shrugging off his shirt, she stepped inside the round tub. *Ahhh.*

Her head rested against the lip of the tub as lavender petals floated around her collarbone. She closed her eyes and relaxed as the warm water soothed her scaling skin and the melodic music played. The meds kicked in, causing her discomfort to subside.

I can get use to a man like this. Preparing her a bath, Braylon had really outdone himself. As soon as he'd found out she was sick, he'd stepped in and taken care of her as if he was her husband, and she loved every minute of it. *You'd make a good husband, Braylon.* Images of three kids running around her and Braylon while outdoors playing in the snow entered her mind. A fine good man like Braylon and three adorable children would be perfect for her, and—

A knock on the door jarred her from her blissful daydream. "Yes," she cooed, opening her eyes.

"Just checking to see if you need anything," his deep voice droned from the other side of the door.

I need you. She slid her hand to her clitoris and caressed it. "I'm good." Now that he'd once licked her into a satisfying orgasm her body couldn't stop yearning for him or his kisses. "I'll be out shortly."

"Just holler if you need me."

"Will do," she said, touching her wet foot to the white rug in front of the tub. She grabbed the towel from the rack near the sink, and as she toweled off something occurred to her—she'd failed to bring clean clothing inside the bathroom. Well, it wasn't like he hadn't seen the best part of her before.

With the damp towel wrapped around her body she stepped out into the living room to find Braylon on the couch reading the newspaper. He lowered the paper from his eyes to gaze at her over the edges. Deep longing spiked in his bright hazel eyes.

"You look fresh." He folded the newspaper and came to stand in front of her.

"I feel fresh."

Dipping his head, he placed a firm hand to her spine. "I've wanted to kiss you all morning." His cool, minty breath fanned her face. Then his hard lips spread over hers, persuading her into a slow, drugging French kiss. His hand trailed down her back and cupped her butt.

Pick me up and take me! her mind rallied.

Sucking her bottom lip, he breathed hotly into her mouth, "It's a good thing I have errands to run."

Yep, that's too bad. I wish you'd stay with me. Maybe someday she'd gain enough courage to verbally express what was on her mind. Feeling like pouting, she asked, "Why's that a good thing?"

He touched a gentle finger to her forehead and trailed it over her cheek down to her lips. "Because I wouldn't be able to keep my hands off you," he pressed his erection against her stomach, "and as soon as you get better I'm going to make love to you."

Cream pooled in her center. "Where are you going?" More than anything she hoped he'd say he'd changed his mind and had decided to stay home, watch a romantic movie with her, and cuddle on the sofa instead. Though he probably liked action ones.

When he clenched the towel her breath accelerated. *Whew!* What would she have done if he'd snatched the thick cloth from her, exposing her nude body? Judging by the way she felt at this moment, she would've let him part her legs and feast on her clitoris exactly like he'd so pleasantly done last night.

Braylon dug in his pocket and pulled out her delivery schedule. "I'm going to deliver your pies for you today," he said, holding the flimsy paper up to her face. Apparently, he'd gotten it off the refrigerator while she'd been showering or asleep this morning. "Then I'm going to check on Royce." He brought his watch up to his face. "And if I have time, I'm going to drop by the youth center to see about volunteering."

The area between her thighs was hot like fire. "Volunteering at the youth center is very kind of you. However, I don't think it's a good idea for you to deliver my pies for me."

His brows furrowed. "I knew you were going to say that."

She rubbed a hand over the wet hair on her nape. "You did?"

He nodded. "Yes, baby. I did. And I know why, too."

"You do?"

"Correct me if I'm wrong, but you're worried about people connecting me to you and the word getting back to your father. Just to let you know, I have big plans for us. No disrespect, but I have no intentions of letting your father get in my way of building a relationship with you. What I want, I get. And what I want...is you."

Whew! My father has finally met his match. "Okay," she said, unhappy with his domineering tone.

"Maybe if he meets me he'll change his mind like you changed yours." He grabbed her hands and squeezed them. "I want to meet your father, Sandella."

She shook her head. "You can't. At least not yet. Maybe someday, but not right now." Because he wanted to meet her father, she questioned how far he planned to take things.

"I understand. But do me a favor and give it some thought. I'd rather meet him first than for him to hear about us in the streets."

Us. So there's an us? A part of her wanted to throw her arms around his neck. And the other part of her wanted to run and hide under a rock. Because getting involved with a Marine could bring about many problems for her. "You have a good point."

Braylon walked to the door, twisted the doorknob, then turned back to face her. "Have you ever thought about selling your pies over the internet? As good as they are, with the right marketing, you'd make a killer profit."

"You really think they're that good?"

His left brow cocked. "I know they are."

She shook her head. "I have no clue how to start an internet business."

"That's what I'm here for. Come up with a company name, and when I get back I can help you begin brainstorming a business plan. That's if you're interested."

Her face broke into a smile. "I'm definitely interested."

After Braylon walked out of the door, she traipsed inside the bedroom and fell flat on her back on top of the mattress. The box springs creaked. She spread open the towel and let the cool temperature connect with her nipples.

For the first time in her life, she felt like she'd finally met the man who God intended to be her husband. It wasn't anything in particular he'd done or said, it was just a gut feeling. Or maybe she was reading too much into his acts of kindness.

He wants to meet Dad. What am I going to do? Is he worth risking my relationship with my father? He makes me feel so incredible.

As she gazed up at the ceiling, the heated night of passion she'd shared with Braylon revisited her mind. Thinking of how his hot tongue had curled over her breasts, her opening tingled. A sensual stormed brewed up inside making her hot all over.

The need to have him inside her to the hilt overwhelmed her. She slid her palm over her hairy mound, pinched her pulsating clitoris. Tugging and pulling at the hard bead…God, she wished it was Braylon's tongue curling over her erected bud, instead of her own twirling fingers.

A hot minute later, her mouth parted and she exploded in her own hand. Smiling and relieved, she rolled to her side and fell fast asleep.

BRAYLON RETURNED TO THE ESTATE two hours later having completed all his errands. As he closed the car to the Jaguar, he wondered if making rounds for Sandella had been the right thing to do. *God, I hope she tells her father about us before someone else does…because whether he likes it or not, I'm going to make sweet love to his daughter.* His balls tingled. *And that's fucking that.*

Sandella's customers seemed shocked when he'd dropped off

the pies at their businesses. Two stylists at the hair salon had even had the nerve to ask him if he was her lover. And when he'd denied the fact, the girl named Sydney had slipped him a torn sheet of paper with her number written on it. The receptionist at the law firm had been no different. Right now he only had eyes for one woman, and that was Sandella, so none of that flirting stuff worked.

Braylon came to a stop in front of Sandella as she lay in the bed, sleeping with a pretty smile on her face, looking like a princess. Her black shiny hair flowed gracefully over her shoulder. The brown skin on her face looked like smooth satin. *You're so damn beautiful.* He could look forever at the sophisticated lady while she slept. But he had other important things to do.

In an effort to not disturb her, he turned and quietly walked out of the room. Inside the kitchen he plopped his laptop on the counter and slid onto the bar stool. He hit a button and the computer zinged to life.

The internet was filled with information on how to start an online bakery as well as how to go about getting a product into major retailers. After thoroughly researching the market, he took the initiative to type up a business plan. He knew it was a little proactive on his behalf, but since he had nothing else to do, he'd decided to help someone as talented as her.

Over two hours had passed when he heard her feet padding across the carpet heading in his direction. "You're finally up, huh?" he said, keeping his eyes trained on the computer.

"I can't believe I slept that long. I must've been tired."

He turned his head and captured her gaze. "Well, you look well rested."

"I am. I hope I'll be able to sleep tonight."

He smiled. "Oh, you will," he said with confidence. Considering how he planned on wearing her out in bed tonight, she needed all the damn sleep she could get.

"I want you to take a look at something." He curved his fingers into her waist and pulled her down on his lap. Heat gathered in his balls. His shaft grew heavy. With his chest pressed to her back, he inhaled the perfumed flowery scent clinging to her flesh.

Maybe he wouldn't wait until tonight to fuck her. Maybe he should pick her up and take her to bed right now. His chest tightened. "I've been working on something for you. Something I hinted at earlier today."

She eyed him sideways then smiled. "You sure stay busy, Mr. Wexler. Do you even remotely know how to relax?"

"Nope. What's resting? I've been told I don't have a lazy bone in my body. Growing up, my father worked the dog out of me and my brothers." He chuckled. "Made us get up at six a.m. even on the weekends to take care of the cattle and tend to the farm. Then we had to go clean his law firm at night."

"That explains your overzealous habits that I find ever so attractive."

"A hard working man is attractive, huh?" He was glad she didn't find his take-charge traits irritating.

"Very." She turned her eyes back to the computer.

"While you were sleep I did some research on starting an online bakery. I saved all the documents and links for you to take a look at once you have the time. I also went ahead and outlined a business plan for you. When you're feeling better we can sit down and finish it together."

Her mouth gaped and she expelled a quick breath. "Other than thank you, I don't know what to say."

"Thank you is more than enough."

"Have you ever thought about starting your own business?"

"No."

"As smart as you are, and as supportive of me, I'm surprised. Did you always want to be a Marine?"

"Yes. And every time I spoke about joining the service to my father he became angry."

"Why?"

"My father had his own dreams for his children. He wanted us to someday work in the law firm with him, and become one of the biggest firms in the nation. While Jaxson and Sonny took to the idea, Caroline and I never did. So after getting my Bachelor's degree I joined the military, and to say he was mad would be an understatement. All my life I'd dreamed of joining the Marines so I followed my own heart instead of his. That's why I understand so well what you're going through with your father. At some point your father is going to have to sever the rope, and let you fly."

She nodded. "Back to me starting a business," she changed the subject. "I'm horrible at technology. Not to mention, I don't have any money to start a thing like this."

"I'm a master when it comes to technology so that's where I come in. I'll teach you everything you need to know in order to run a successful business. Once you learn the ins and outs, it'll be a piece of cake." He dragged the mouse up to the top of the business plan. "Did you give any thought while I was gone about what you'd like to name it?"

"I tried, but nothing seemed to stick."

"Hmmm." His index finger shot up in the air. "How about you name it after your parents?"

"Huh?"

"SugarKanes Bakery & Sweet Shop," he said, wrapping his arms around her waist, stroking the pads of his fingers over the computer's keypad.

"SugarKanes Bakery & Sweet Shop," she said. "That's it! It's perfect! Just simply perfect!" She clapped her hands in front of her face. She then cupped his jaws. "You're a genius!"

"I'm far from that. I'm good at designing websites, but we can work on that tomorrow or the day after."

Suddenly, her eyes misted. "I love the name you came up with. You're so creative, and I just know my brothers will love it just as much as I do. As soon as I get my first order, I'm going to pay you something for helping me."

"You don't have to pay me, Sandella. You deserve—"

She put a finger to his mouth. "Shhhh." She pressed her tongue into his mouth and started kissing him feverishly.

A groan sounded deep inside his larynx. "I can think of better ways for you to repay me, baby." *My dick can, too.*

She giggled, then nipped his bottom lip. "I'm going to make you so proud of me. SugarKanes is going to be a hit."

Speaking of hit…if you just let me hit that pussy that'll be more than enough for me. He fisted her hair and thrust his tongue inside her mouth. As he savored her tongue, he noticed the inside of her mouth seemed rather hot. His mouth stilled, and he placed a hand to her forehead.

"My sweet baby, you're hot."

Hanging on to his gaze, she blinked sexily at him, then twirled the ends of her hair around her finger. "Why, thank you, cowboy," she teased.

"No, I'm serious." He touched her reddening cheeks. "Your skin is burning up. It's time for you to get back in bed." He grabbed her palm and led her toward the bedroom.

"But I just woke up." She pouted. "And I'm not sleepy."

"You don't have to go back to sleep, but you do need to lie down. If you feel up to it, I'd be more than happy to try and eat that fever right on out of you like I did last night. How does that sound?"

Shit. He had to do something to get his jollies off. If he didn't, he was going to burst all over the damn place. Licking her was the only answer from where he stood. Of course, he'd love to fuck her.

But the last thing he needed was to make her temperature rise even higher by pounding her into a fulfilling orgasm.

When they reached the room, Sandella lay back on the bed. "I'm all yours," she cooed, spreading her legs, and sounding better than she really was.

He pushed her panties to the side and drove his tongue into her sweet cherry entrance. The tip of his tongue traced the circle of her hot sex. She squirmed, fisted the sheets. As her aroused whimpering filled his ears her slick wet heat dripped onto his probing flesh, filling his mouth with her powerful orgasm. *Fuck! This is the best tasting pussy in the whole damn world.* He drank the feverish liquid squirting on his tongue like a tall glass of wine.

"Oh, Braylon." She sang his name like a gentle love song.

Chapter Six

BRAYLON STOOD AT THE MIRROR inside his bedroom buttoning up his long-sleeve dress shirt, cursing himself for falling so hard for Sandella. He hefted the bottle of cologne and squirted both sides of his neck. *How in the hell did I let this happen?* Wouldn't it be nice if the reflection staring back at him could figure the question out?

Over the last few days he'd taken great pleasure in helping nurse Sandella back to health. He'd done his best to take care of her every need. During the time she'd been ill, they'd shared several intimate moments together. But they'd spent majority of the time talking and cuddling. His behavior had surprised him because he damn sure wasn't the cuddling type. Until he'd met her, he'd never even imagined engaging in such sensual behaviors.

Watching romance movies, Lord help me. Talk about boring. He'd even sat his ass on the sofa with her and watched the freaking soap operas, something he'd only done for the sake of making her happy, and just to spend time with her. This damn woman had made a move on his heart, and after breaking up with the snooty

Madison, he'd vowed he'd never be vulnerable to a woman again.

As he raked the comb one last time through his hair, he cursed. Sandella had him hooked. He adjusted his collar. And now it was time for him to hook her, brand her, and take things to the next level. He hoped she liked what he'd planned for her this evening.

Yesterday he'd placed an invitation in the mailbox for her to join him in the backyard of the estate for a romantic dinner. As soon as she'd retrieved and read the invitation, she'd found him in the cottage and had run up to him, kissing all over his face as if he were taking her to an upscale expensive restaurant or flying her somewhere like London. She'd been impressed by his willingness to take time to actually print the invite out on the computer, too.

Simple things excited her, not his wealth or lack thereof, and that's what he liked about her. So often the women he'd dated in the past had wasted no time to jump on the computer to Google him and the history of his family. And when they'd found out he was the son of a very wealthy attorney, who along with his brother had established Wexler & Wexler Attorneys at Law—a large firm out in Texas with branches in the southern states as well—they'd seemed to become even more interested. One chick even had the nerve to tell him he was stupid for being a Marine when he could go work for his father. As if his father thinking he was stupid wasn't enough.

His cell buzzed. "Hello," he answered, before looking at the screen.

"Oh good. You answered," Madison said.

"How are you, Madison?"

"Good."

"And Drayton?"

"He's not doing too well. And that's why I'm calling. Ever since he met you and knows you're his father, he keeps crying for you at night. He misses his daddy. Is there any way you can come see him?"

Trying to keep a level head, he suppressed his raging fury with Madison. She'd known all along that Drayton was his, and should've never kept this precious boy from him. And now she expected him to just jump into the boy's life and start playing daddy? While he'd love nothing more than to engage in a fatherly role, he wasn't about to until she agreed to a paternity test.

"Have you scheduled the paternity test yet?"

"Yes. It's slated for three weeks from now."

"Then I'll see Drayton when I arrive at that time."

"Would you like to speak with him? He's right here."

"I can't right now. I was just on my way out the door."

Madison released an agitated breath. "Fine. Good night," she said, disconnecting the call.

Shit. He spied the alarm clock to find it was fifteen minutes before eight. After he slid his black trousers over his hips, he stuffed his shirt inside his pants and zipped them. He gave himself a once-over in the mirror, walked through the living room, then stepped outside into the cool evening air. He'd made every attempt to make sure his first time with Sandella was going to be a memorable night for her.

His eyes scanned the landscape of the backyard. The rental company had done a great job setting up for his personal event. Five torches lined both sides of the concrete and blazed with orange fire. And up under the tent were a small circular table and two chairs overlooking the river. *I can't believe I did all of this. Shit, she may think I'm about to ask her to marry me. Oh hell no, I ain't whipped. Can't be. Ain't even had any pussy yet.*

As Braylon stood beside the garage, Sandella's rattling car rolled up the driveway. He walked up to the driver's side and politely opened the door for her. When she slid out of the car and stepped onto the pavement, his heart thudded in his throat. His tool pulsated. The sight of her stole his breath.

She wore a thin, ivory sweater dress stopping right above her knees. A strand of pearls draped elegantly around her slender neck. Her long hair was pulled back into a tight low bun with curly bangs falling down on both sides of her delicate face. And a light pink gloss painted her kissable lips.

Inhaling the enticing peachy fragrance of her body, he kissed her cheek. "You look stunning, Sandella."

Her lips curved up into a blinding white smile. "Thank you. You look nice, too."

"Thanks." *Maybe I should've said hi to Drayton.*

Her gaze roved over the backyard. "Oh my goodness." Both her hands pressed flat to her chest. "Is all of this for me?" She tilted her head back, looking up at him.

"Yes. I wanted to make this night very special for you." He took her hand. "One that you'll never forget."

SANDELLA'S HEART REJOICED AS BRAYLON escorted her between the blazing fire torches on either side of the concrete. A white tent beside her favorite oak tree sat close to the river. The cool night air fluffed against her face while the gentle wind swirling from the river prickled her scalp.

God, this is so romantic. No one has ever done anything like this for me before. What did I ever do to deserve this? She lifted her gaze to the half-moon radiating in the dark evening sky, then turned to look at Braylon. Appreciating his hard efforts, she smiled inwardly.

After they reached the tent, he pulled the chair draped in ivory fabric and tied with a gold tassel out from beneath the table. She smoothed her hands over the material covering her buttocks, taking a seat. Braylon rounded the table and sat across from her.

A red, burning candle sat centered on top of the white tablecloth, but nothing else. He pulled his cell phone from his pants, tapped the screen, then placed it to his ear. "We're ready." He hung up.

"Ready for what?"

"Dinner," he said, sliding the cell back into its clip.

"You sure know how to make it hard for a girl to resist you, don't you?"

"Believe it or not, this is my first time putting together something like this."

"Well, you've done a great job, and I'm flattered. This is absolutely beautiful...just beautiful, Braylon."

"Since I can't cook, I hired a chef to do the cooking for me," he admitted.

She tilted her head. "Ahh. You shouldn't have gone through all the trouble. I would've been fine if you just picked up something."

A tall Caucasian man wearing a white apron appeared in the back doorway of the main house. Carrying a tray in his opened hand, he walked across the lawn then came to stand in front of them. He lowered a covered dish in front of Sandella first, then he sat one in front of Braylon. After putting the circular serving tray to the side, he took both hands and lifted their lids simultaneously.

Sandella's mouth watered as she inhaled the tasty-looking meal. There was grilled lobster tail, fresh sautéed creek shrimp, lemon herb roasted potatoes, and a small green salad with walnuts.

The waiter lifted the bottle of German Riesling out of the bucket of ice perched on the stand, filled their glasses, then disappeared.

She unfurled her napkin and placed it in her lap. "This looks delicious."

"I remembered you saying you loved seafood. I hope you enjoy it."

Just being with you is plenty. "I'm sure I will."

He hefted his glass to the air. "I'd like to make a toast."

"Go ahead," she said, holding her glass in front of her face.

"To friendship." *Friends? Is that all we are?* He continued. "As we become better acquainted, may our friendship continue to grow stronger." Their glasses clinked. *What about becoming serious? Or perhaps lovers?* she halfway wanted to ask, but didn't.

As she looked across the table at him her heart swelled. *What a nice friend I have.* "Nice toast." Sipping the wine, the immense sweet flavor bubbled on her tongue.

"Nice lady." Retrieving his cell, he thumbed over the screen, hit a button, then lowered it to the table in front of the burning red candle. Smooth sounds of whimsical jazz infiltrated her ears.

The conversation between them flowed easy and free during dinner. She carved a chunk of lobster out of the shell. "What's the name of this song?"

"A Mid Autumn Night's Dream." Holding the fork to his mouth, he bit into the shrimp.

"Perfect title for an evening like this." The warm lobster lay on her tongue and she savored the juicy, tender meat.

"Yes it is. I have my own autumn night dream that I'm hoping to fulfill by the time this evening is over."

"And what's that?" She wondered what her expression looked like to him.

He extended his arm across the table and took her hand. "I want to make love to you." Desire rushed through her body.

Her tingly nipples balled up. "I'd like that." *Should I tell him I'm a virgin? No. The conversation alone may ruin the mood.*

His hazel eyes flickered like a Christmas tree at her agreement. Braylon wiped his mouth, pushed back his chair, and stood. His figure towered her as he reached down for her hand, gesturing her to stand. He draped an arm around her waist, drew her to him.

"Let's dance."

When she palmed his shoulder, he grabbed her free hand and leveled their clenching hands to her shoulder. Their bodies swayed sensually beneath the oak to the jazz overture in the background. Her breasts up against his muscular pectoris felt like heaven.

As they danced she cradled her head to his chest, absorbing the breathtaking view of the fierce torches burning in the distance. She closed her eyes and let herself sink into the hard contours of his body. His penis grinding against her abdomen turned to steel. *Uh oh. He's ready for me.*

He stopped swaying, cupped her neck. "I'm ready to make love to you," he groaned, a deep longing for sex glittering in his eyes.

She swallowed. Heat shot through her veins like slick lava. Her vagina clenched then dripped fluid into her panties. *I'm melting.* "I'm ready, too."

He yanked her off her feet and walked across the lawn toward the guest cottage. "I couldn't think of a better dessert." He dipped his head then placed a burning kiss on her lips.

I'm his dessert. Oh my, my my. She'd never engaged in sexual intercourse to the point of penetration before. She prayed to God that she didn't disappoint him.

Her head fit perfectly in the hollow between his shoulder and neck as he carried her through the sparkly orange torches. The warmth of his arms was so male, so bracing. His woody masculine scent tantalized her.

He pushed open the door of the cottage, stepped over the threshold, kicked the door closed behind him, then headed straight to the master bedroom.

Coming to a stop at the foot of the bed, he lowered her to her feet. With a finger to her chin, he palmed the back of her head. "I can't wait to be inside of you." He trailed a gentle finger over her lips.

His penis feels so heavy on my stomach. Good gracious, he's going to split me wide open. She swallowed the insecurity bubbling at the base of her throat.

His seductive gaze slid downward to her breasts, then his mouth covered hers hungrily. The caress of his lips gliding over hers set her aflame. He began to tenderly massage her buttocks.

"Touch me." Before she had the chance to respond, he grabbed her hand, slid it inside his pants, and put it on his hard member.

Dear Lord. Surprise shot through her as his erection jutted into her clutched palm like a humongous vibrator. *He's huge, very huge.*

More heat oozed into her entrance. She squeezed him hard then stroked him up and down. Merging her tongue with his, she drank his groans into her mouth.

He grabbed her dress at the hem, rolled it up over her head. Her hair fell from the up-do to her shoulders. He ran a finger over the fabric of her bra, pinching her erect nipple. "You're so beautiful. And tonight, you're mine. Say you're mine," he ordered, unfastening her bra.

"I'm yours, Braylon. All yours," she cooed as her bra fell from her shoulders to the floor.

He hooked his fingers at the waistline of her panties. Rolling them down the length of her legs, he crouched. Although she was sure about her readiness to give herself to him a sense of uneasiness settled in the pit of her stomach. *This is the perfect man to lose my virginity to.*

With his hands kneading her bare butt, he gently circled the tip of his nose against the patch of black hair covering her hot sex, and sniffed. "Mmmm," he moaned. "Let me taste your pussy."

When his fingers touched her, she shivered. He parted her quivering labia and pressed his tongue inside her. Finding her G-spot, he thrashed against the sensitive nerves and licked her something delicious. Grabbing the top of his head, her head rolled backward. She bit back the harsh whimper threatening to erupt from her mouth.

Leaving her clitoris, he rose slowly. Braylon palmed her hips and lapped his thick tongue over her navel, then flicked it over her nipple. She cried out in pleasure.

Pinning her with a seductive stare, his fingers undid the buttons at the top of his dress shirt while she worked quickly to undo the buttons at the bottom. As she removed his shirt, he unbuckled his belt. When he rolled his pants and underwear down his muscular legs, his erect cock plopped out.

He swept her tongue from her mouth back into his. The feel of his bare erection gliding across her belly sent shock waves of electricity charging to her brain. She wondered how much more she could stand.

With their mouths feasting hungrily, he lowered her to the mattress. Sensation brewed inside her veins like a boiling caffeinated latte. She was really going to do this, she thought. Her first time would hurt but she didn't care. Rummaging her fingers wildly through his hair, she circled her hips, grinding against his tool.

He lifted her to place a pillow beneath her buttocks. Braylon spread her legs wide, clenched his erection with his fingers, then put his head on her wet opening. She prepared for him to brand her, tense beneath his hard physique.

"Open your eyes, Sandella," he groaned. Her right eye popped open. "Both of them." There went the left one. "I want to see your eyes as I sink to the bottom of you." As wet as she was he was sure to drown at some point, she thought.

He slowly inched the top half of his thick shaft inside. Her constricted walls stretched. His girth was thick and fulfilling to the point it seemed inhuman. Receiving him, she fisted the sheets. She bit gently at the inside of her cheeks as a low grunt sat on the opening of her lips dying to escape.

Rocking his hips, he paused. Concern enveloped his pupils. "Damn, you're tight. Are you a virgin?"

Nodding, she purred, "Yes, Braylon. You're my first."

"Fuck!" He jumped off her and rolled out of bed to his feet.

Mortified, she rose up on her elbows.

He grasped the sides of his head. "You didn't tell me you were a virgin!"

BRAYLON'S SHAFT THROBBED AND FELT ready to burst on him as he paced back and forth at the side of the bed, trying to make an acute decision. Both his brain and his cock were troubled, on the verge of hurting. The naked, sexy lady in his bed had just told him she was a fucking virgin, that he was her first. He paused and looked down at Sandella. *Jesus Christ. What's a man to do?*

Her virginity was indeed a problem for him because he had a tendency to fuck women then not want to be bothered with them after doing so. And the last thing he wanted was to do that to someone as sweet and as special as Sandella. Damn, why didn't he have this conversation beforehand? Admiring the round curves of her swollen breasts and her pointed black nipples, the squirming balls in his sac rolled into knots. *Ouch.*

She tilted her chin to look up at him. The bluish moon glowed through the slits in the blinds over her soft circular face. Batting her eyelashes, her rounded eyes gleamed with arousal. "I didn't know I had to tell you."

He released a pent-up breath. "Are you sure you want to do this?"

She flattened her hands on the mattress, spread her legs wider. "I'm positive. And just so you know...I've been ready for quite some time now." She slid her finger in her mouth and sucked it.

Electricity surged through his throbbing shaft. He flew on top of her, and she fell flat on her back. Fondling the hot space between her legs, he found her tender entrance then reinserted himself into her creamy wetlands.

When she wrapped her legs around his waist she bucked, forcing him to slip to the bottom of her. *Fucking Christ!* Her tight walls clenched him like a slick glove as he stroked.

He slid his pulsating shaft to her entrance, leaving just the tip in, then slowly pressed back down. He moaned. "You feel so good, Sandella."

SOFT COOS CAME FROM SANDELLA'S pursed lips. "You too." Now that the pain had subsided Braylon's skillful penetration was bringing her sheer pleasure. *Mmmm, he's hitting all the right spots.* As he sucked her sensitive areola, she tucked her body into his contours and grabbed his butt. So many pleasures at once, *oh my.*

Their sweaty bodies were in exquisite harmony with one another as he moved in and out of her, urging her toward an orgasm. Their eyes locked. Her shallow breathing quickened. Approaching her climax, her sex beat fiercely.

He brought his member up to her entrance again, and when he slammed back in an orgasm rippled through her body. "Braylon!" A rush of wild wind expelled from her lungs as she yelled out his name.

He dipped up and down. He shuddered. "I feel your pussy exploding on my dick. You're making me come, baby." His back straightened. He continued to stroke her as hot sperm squirted inside, filling her to the hilt.

Now that was good. I'm in love. Her body hadn't had the chance to recuperate and here she wanted to do it again already.

A satisfied glow filled his eyes as he pecked her forehead. Taking in every little detail of their lovemaking aftermath, she felt his cock soften inside her. He rolled off her. She smiled outwardly and inwardly.

"Come here, baby." He gathered her in his arms.

Sandella's thighs felt sticky as she lay cuddled up against his chest. "I'm so glad you were my first."

With his chest pressing into her back, and his penis against her butt, he caressed her arm. "Me too, Sandella. Me too." He bestowed the back of her head with a kiss. Shortly thereafter, Sandella drifted off to sleep satisfied, and in the bulky arms of a fine Marine.

Chapter Seven

EARLY THE NEXT MORNING, THE loud engine of a motor boat strummed inside Braylon's ears and awakened him from a deep slumber. He stirred, then opened his eyes to find his limbs were entangled with Sandella's. Her naked left leg was thrown over his hip and her arm was strewn across his chest.

God she was so beautiful when she slept. As the sound of the motor faded, he thought back to the way he'd made love to her last night. His heart stirred remembering that he'd been her first. *I got that pussy first.*

He mentally raised a fist in the air as if he were a boxing champion. Smiling, he rubbed a hand over his chest. What he felt for her was so different than anything he'd ever experienced before.

Braylon laced his fingers together behind his head and stared at the ceiling. His movement jarred Sandella out of her sleep. She peeled her eyes open. "Good morning…beautiful," he said.

"Good morning." She snuggled up tighter to him then lay her head on his chest.

He lowered his arm to cup her shoulder. "Last night was the

best night of my life."

She smiled. "It was the most beautiful night for me, too." She ran a finger over a deep gash to the right of his navel. "How'd you get this scar?"

"I was shot while serving on the front line in Iraq. I almost died."

She eased up in bed. "You fought in the war? Willa never mentioned it to me."

"That's because she didn't know. My father and I decided it'd be best not to tell her. We didn't want her worrying. But as soon as she returns I'm going to tell her."

"She'll be shocked."

"Probably mad that we didn't tell her, too."

"I've never known anyone who fought in a war before. I want to hear all about it. Were you scared?"

He propped a pillow up against the headboard behind his back and another one in his lap. He patted the pillow in his lap. "Lay your head here and I'll tell you all about it."

When she nestled her head on the pillow, long black strands of hair toppled over her face. He scooped up her tresses, arranging them to parade down her spine.

Bloody images of Iraq surfaced in his brain. His heart squeezed. Losing many of his friends during the terrible war had devastated him. He'd thought he was going to die out in that damn desert. God damn it felt good to be in Hilton Head Island smitten by a pretty lady and getting some good pussy.

"I'm so glad you're willing and wanting to listen to my experience in the war. It really helps when I talk about it with someone who truly cares." Braylon's mind flashed back to Madison. After he returned home three years ago, Madison had never wanted to listen to him talk about Iraq. The spoiled, snobbish lady was too wrapped up into herself to even care about the horrors he'd been through. When Braylon had asked about taking their relationship to the next level, she'd flat out said his career chosen path as a Marine didn't fit her family's image of what they wanted her husband to be.

She pushed him to go back to law school and work in his father's business. Finally, he'd gotten so fed up with Madison trying to change him, he dumped her. And now she claimed they shared a son. *Drayton. What am I going to do when I find out Drayton's really mine?*

He sulked inwardly then shifted his views back to Iraq. Every time he revisited that time in his life he felt like crying. And although he never wept outwardly, his heart wept inside on a regular basis. The macho side of him fought to keep his wounded heart a secret.

"When my squad first arrived at our outpost in Iraq, the first thing we did was outfit our living quarters." He drifted away.

Growing up in the comforts of a luxurious Texas-style mansion, outfitting his living quarters hadn't come easy for Braylon upon his arrival in Iraq. Back home a person just stayed inside if the weather was unrelenting, but in the desert he had to salvage wood to build shelter against the vicious winds. While pissing into metal pipe fed through a barricade filled with dirt was challenging, it'd been even harder for him to burn his own feces in a metal drum.

Forget about taking a shower because there wasn't any running water. After long days of gruesome foot patrolling the infantrymen would pull on new socks, use baby wipes to clean their bodies, and smother themselves in baby powder so they could pretend they smelled decent.

"It was misery, but we endured the misery together."

Sandella sat upright. "How do you feel about women fighting on the front lines?"

"While I think women are more than qualified to fight, I have mixed feelings about it."

"Why's that?"

"As men, we fight together, kill together, and get killed together. And while that bothers me, I think I'd react differently and be worse off if I saw a woman fighting next to me get her head blown off. I also think I'd be more inclined to help a woman who'd been injured before I helped a man." *And some men can't focus with titties and a fine piece of ass around them.*

"Yeah, I see your point."

Tears streamed down her face after he shared the fact that everyone in his unit except for him had died after a bomb explosion. "I'm glad to have served my country. If I had to do it all over again, I wouldn't change a thing. I'm proud to be a Marine," he said, emphasizing the word Marine, getting out of bed.

He opened the closet door, retrieved a box full of photos from the shelf, then made his way back to the bed. "This is a picture of me and the men in my unit," he said, handing her the photo filled with brave Marines.

She slid the picture he'd given her to the back of the rest to look at the following one. The skin at the corner of her eyes compressed as she peered down at the photo of him sitting next to body bags. She glanced up at him. "This is so sad. I'm so sorry." Her eyes misted. "I'm so proud of you. Thank you for everything you've done for this country." She threw her arms around his neck and kissed him as if he didn't have early morning breath.

As his tongue twirled around hers, his cock stiffened. He motioned her to her back, threw her sultry legs over his shoulders, and drove his tool inside the sweet juices of her juncture.

Riding her, he cupped the heel of her foot and kissed it. *I'm never going to tire of this pussy.* He might not be ready to admit it, but this damn woman had a hold on him.

Gyrating her hips, she placed her toes on his lips, and he sucked the two big ones inside his mouth. She burst into laughter. "That tickles!"

Stroke. Stroke. "It does, huh?" With his fingers grasping her ankles, he stroked her and suckled on her toes like they were stick candy.

"Stop! I can't take it!" She covered her mouth and couldn't stop laughing.

"You're tickling me, too" he thrust into her, "so it's only fair that I tickle you back." Rocking his hips back and forth, he tortured her cute pink-painted toes.

Giggling, she hefted the pillow from the headboard, tossed it in his face. She then gyrated her hips, intentionally severing their connection, and rolled out of bed to her feet. She stood at the side of the bed with her arms wrapped around her waist, cracking up with girlish laughter. Witnessing firsthand her extreme excitement, he became aroused to the point of no return.

He clambered out of bed, walked to the back of her, and then reached around to caress the high swells of her breasts. Grinding his erection against her spine, he slid a hand between her legs and pinched her clitoris. Her laughter turned into deep, intense gasps.

He placed a hand on her spine, grabbed hiserection, then rubbed his mushroom head along the crack of her butt. "I'm going to take you from behind."

Following his lead, she flattened her hands on the rumpled linen, bent over, and he slid his shaft deep inside her. *Oh yeah. This pussy will always be mine.*

MAKING GOOD LOVE TO SANDELLA twice this morning had Braylon rushing to get to work. He glanced at the clock inside the Hummer then cursed. An extremist when it came to punctuality, he'd never been late to work before and had no intentions of being tardy today either. Appreciating the durability of his SUV, he weaved around a slow-moving Pontiac and made a quick right into Parris Island military base.

Reaching the guard's station, he halted. The guard stared at him, then after scrutinizing his ID saluted him. Braylon raised his hand to his forehead saluting him in return. The security on the base was airtight, just like it should be.

The long road leading to his office had a cozy country feeling. Large oaks with huge branches draped with grey moss lined both sides of the road. A smiled covered his face as he cruised past recruits jogging alongside the road, dressed in camouflage and spit-shined boots. The drill sergeant chanting out in front curved to his right with his team of recruits strictly following his lead.

Braylon wheeled his truck in front of the brick building, parked, and read the time on the dashboard. Good, he was fifteen minutes early. Because he liked to arrive to work at least thirty minutes beforehand, he and Sandella were going to have to start having sex earlier in the morning from now on.

The fall sun beat down on his nape as he climbed the steps of the building. He pulled the door open and gladly stepped inside. After three and a half weeks of relaxing, it sure felt good to finally start work, he thought, taking in his professional surroundings.

Marines walked about inside the office wearing various forms of uniforms, depending on their ranks and assigned duties. He'd already had the pleasure of meeting his boss, Spencer Knox, the same day as he'd met Sandella so he knew exactly where his office was.

As he strode down the hallway toward Spencer's office, an attractive blond female dressed in navy blues stopped him. "Do you need help?" she asked, her eyes raking over his body. Was this woman coming on to him? Did she have the nerve to flirt with him on their first meeting?

"Thanks, but I'm good."

"Well, if you ever need anything," she looked back over her shoulder, then back at him, "I'm Alyssa...Alyssa Carrington." She extended her arm.

Braylon shook her hand. "Braylon Wexler. Nice meeting you, Alyssa."

"No, it's nice meeting you," she said, emphasizing the *you*. "Mmm. Mmm. Mmm," she hummed, strutting off.

When Braylon turned around to look at the sexy blond, she was looking back at him too. He smiled, then proceeded toward his destination. *Sorry, Alyssa, I'm taken.* The sudden thought of belonging to only one woman, Sandella, had come out of nowhere and nearly scared the living shit out of him.

He emerged inside the office of his boss, Lieutenant Colonel Spencer Knox, to find him standing behind his desk, looking out the window. Braylon cleared his throat. "Good morning."

Spencer's head snapped in his direction. He looked down at the clock on his desk then back at Braylon. "Good morning. For a second there I thought you'd be late. Just so you know, I have low tolerance for tardiness." He chuckled dryly.

Braylon detected a condescending tone in the man's voice. "Well, it's a good thing I'm right on time." *If it hadn't been for making love to Sandella I would've been much earlier.*

A tall lanky white man with thick brown eyebrows marched into Spencer's office and came to a stop next to Braylon. "You must be our new Criminal Investigator...Braylon Wexler."

Damn, his eyebrows need trimming. "Yes. I am."

"I'm Lieutenant Colonel Forest Greene." Braylon's brows must've hitched. "Yeah, yeah, I know. It's a dumb name, but you can blame my momma for that." Forest burst into laughter and Spencer joined him. "Who the hell knows, maybe the broad was pissy drunk when she had me. That'd explain my behavior, wouldn't it, Knox?"

"If you say so." Spencer said, shaking his head.

Braylon found Forest's untimely remark and tone rather unprofessional considering this was their first meeting. Maybe he was just too uptight because he'd been on edge about possibly running late.

"Anyway, welcome to Parris Island. My office is right down the hallway. Let me know if I can be of any help to you. Nice meeting you."

"Likewise."

Spencer said, "I'll show you around, introduce you to your coworkers, then you can get settled and began your day."

HOURS LATER AFTER SPENCER SHOWED Braylon around the base, he returned to his office. He plopped down in his chair and hit the button on his computer. Rolling his shoulders, he sighed, then leaned back in his chair waiting for the computer to charge up. All that great sex last night and this morning had him longing for some more. He thought about Sandella and his manhood hardened.

His eyes scanned over the clean spacious workspace. *Nice office. It's much different than being on the front lines of a war.* He folded his arms across his chest and noticed the blinking red light on his desk phone. He had a message.

He lifted the phone to his ear, hit the inbox for his voicemail, and grabbed a pen from his organizer. In search of a note pad to write on, he pulled open his desk drawer and found several pieces of unopened mail inside. One of the envelopes was stamped *confidential* in red. *Confidential?* He hefted the medium brown envelope along with a yellow Post-it.

"Hi Braylon, this is Alyssa." *Alyssa? Oh yeah, the girl I met in the hallway this morning.* "I forgot to give you my number. It's

551-1352. Again…551-1352. Call me sometime." Braylon smiled at the woman's determination and dropped the receiver back on its base. Because he had no intention of calling her, he didn't bother to write down her number. Right now his mind was on one woman, and one woman only. Sandella.

Assuming the envelope had belonged to the individual that had had this office before him, he flipped it over, slid his finger under the flap, and broke the seal. He pulled out a sheet of paper with a typewritten message addressed to him. As he read over the unnerving document, his heart scrambled like eggs inside his chest. The letter read:

Dear Detective Wexler.

Inside this envelope is the original case file documenting the death of Sugar Summers. I'm acutely aware that you know the deceased woman's daughter, Sandella, and thought this might be of high interest to you. Considering you are the new lead Criminal Investigator for Parris Island, I'd think finding her killer would be of utmost importance.

While I'd much rather speak to you in person than write this letter, I'm smart enough to know that it wouldn't prove wise. The last man that attempted to do such a thing was found murdered in the woods. With that being said, I'm pleading with you to please reopen the case and bring him down. All of the answers pertaining to Sugar's untimely and unfortunate death can be found right under your nose if you sniff hard enough.

Welcome to Parris Island,
Simon

Fucking Christ! Braylon scampered briskly across the room and shut the door. With his heart beating like a drum against his chest, he flopped down in his chair, and pulled out the remainder of the contents inside the envelope. He grasped the police report as sweat beaded on his forehead.

He swiped at the sweat then reclined in the chair. *Dear God.* When he flipped to the second page he almost pissed on himself. In his hands was a bloody image of Sandella's mother taken right after she'd died.

Who's Simon? he wondered, rereading the signature at the bottom of the letter. He had no idea who Simon was, but he damn sure planned to find out. And now that someone had felt it necessary that he take a look at Sandella's mother's case, he was going to try his damndest to find out who her killer was. He locked the file in his drawer then pondered what to do next.

Sliding the key to the lock inside his pocket, he crossed the room to the door and made his way over to his secretary's, Victoria's, desk. How this shit had been thrown in his lap his first day was kind of scary. Downright creepy. Who in the hell knew about him and Sandella? Could this Simon guy be the killer?

Victoria, a brunette with short wavy hair, lifted her eyes from the computer screen. Her lips curved upward. "How's your first day going?" She popped a breath mint in her mouth.

Crazy as fuck. "It's going great." He leaned into her. "Do you by any chance know an employee by the name of Simon?"

Victoria's brows creased. Thinking, she fisted her chin. "No, sorry. The name Simon doesn't ring a bell, but if you give me a last name I can check the database for you to find out who he is?"

The last thing he needed to do was to get Victoria involved in something this dangerous. "No, that's okay." He'd find out who Simon was on his own.

He thanked Victoria for offering to help him, turned on the soles of his shoes, and returned to his office. After unlocking his desk drawer, he tucked the file regarding Sugar under his armpit, then made his way toward his Hummer. The cool afternoon air rustled against his face as he descended the steps. He clambered in his SUV and cranked the engine.

As he touched the steering wheel the image of Sugar's bloody, lifeless body flashed inside his head. A part of him wished he'd never seen the photos. Tension knotted his shoulders.

Settling back against the seat, he shut his eyes, then reopened them. *Who the fuck is Simon?* He shifted the car into drive and pulled out of the lot. Driving down the long road lined with huge oaks, his mind shifted to Sandella. Until he got to the bottom of this, he had to protect her from knowing, he thought, passing the guard's station.

INSIDE THE MAIN HOUSE SANDELLA watched Royce climb beneath the covers of his bed. "I'm so glad you're back, Royce."

"I'm back," he said, pulling the linen up to his chin.

"Good night."

He rolled on his side. "Night, night." Yawning, he shut his eyes.

Sandella flicked off the lights, rounded the corner, and strolled inside the guest bedroom where she was now staying again. Although she was glad Royce had returned, she was sure going to miss sleeping in Braylon's bed. And waking up to his handsome face every morning.

She drew back the drapery shielding the window and peered down at the guest cottage. The light in the foyer clicked off. Because she missed Braylon and had some great news to share with him, she sure hoped he was on his way up to see her. Having showered earlier, she pulled a nightgown from the drawer and slid it over her head.

With her back turned toward the mirror, she looked over her shoulder to glance at herself. The peach silk fabric dipped low in the back and clung to her figure. Willa would probably disfavor her wearing the elegant, seductive gown inside her house. *I wonder how Willa and Drake are going to feel about me dating Braylon?*

She was in way over her head. He'd never said they were dating. In fact, he'd stated they were just friends. *Friends, huh? Friends have no business doing what we've been doing.*

Sandella slid her feet into a pair of white furry slippers and shrugged on her matching peach silk robe. Her hand glided along the rail of the staircase as she descended the steps. She glanced around the kitchen in search of Braylon, but he wasn't there. After all that wild sex they'd had this morning and considering today had been his first day of work, you'd think he'd at least come see her. Disappointed, she folded her arms across her breasts.

After waiting at the table another ten minutes for him to show up, annoyance brewed like boiling liquid inside her. The least he could've done was come say hi. Or I miss you. Or how was your day? Was it possible he'd gone to bed without coming to kiss her good night? Even though she'd wanted more than just a kiss from him.

A frustrated breath expelled from her mouth. She felt her lips pouting. *That's it!* She scooted back the chair, padded across the plush carpet of the living room, and stormed out the side door.

Sandella stood on the step of the cottage knotting the sash on her silk robe. The door cracked open. As soon as their gazes connected her pent-up frustration dissolved.

Braylon wore a tight navy shirt and white sweatpants. "I was just coming to see you." His lips curled upward.

Well, you're too slow. "You were?"

"Yes, I've been thinking about doing this." He dropped his head to hers, letting his lips linger above her slightly parted mouth. "All day." He slid his tongue inside her mouth kissing her intimately. God, she loved kissing him, she thought, moving her tongue with his. Sizzling heat shot straight to her core.

He broke their kiss and she walked in. He flicked on the light and boldly assessed her. A sheen of light glistened in his eyes like he cared deeply for her.

The tremendous success revolving around SugarKanes caused her to smile. "I have some great news to share with you."

"What's that?"

Ecstatic, she inhaled a deep breath. "SugarKanes sold two hundred pies this week!"

"Seven hundred? That's great! I knew you could do it. I bet the numbers are going to double, maybe even triple, by the end of next week. You're destined for greatness, baby."

"You think so?"

He swiped a finger over her chin. "I know so."

Blushing, her eyes transferred from his face to the counter. A brown envelope sat on top on his laptop. "I see you brought your work home with you."

He looked back at the envelope then back at her. A dull light settled in his eyes. "Oh, that's nothing. I was just reviewing a case."

"You got your first case already! Ooo. Let me see!" When she went toward the file, he grabbed her elbow. He spun her around.

"My work has to remain confidential. Don't go near it."

She stuck out her lower lip. "Ahh. Can't you just give me a little hint about your first investigation?"

He draped an arm around her waist and drew her to him. "No. I'm sorry, I can't." His hand ran up and down the silky fabric covering her back. "The color peach looks nice on you."

"Thanks." His job as a criminal investigator for the Marines really interested her. Darn…she really wanted to know what his first case was all about.

"I must say I'm a little disappointed that you've already taken your bath because I was hoping to bathe you." He put a finger to her cheek. "I'll do it after I make love to you," he said, unknotting her robe.

She grabbed his wrists. "Royce is back."

"He is?"

"Yes. I picked him up today."

"That's good." His fingers worked diligently at the knot on her sash. "You smell good," he said, inhaling the cherry mist she'd sprayed on her neck right before walking downstairs.

"I've got to get back to the main house. Royce will have a fit if he wakes up and I'm not there."

Ignoring her, Braylon jerked her off her feet. "He'll be just fine for the next fifteen minutes." He strode inside the master bedroom and lowered her to the bed.

Unable to resist him, she hiked her gown up to her hips and spread her legs. "Can you make that five minutes instead?"

"As hard as my cock is, I can make it two." He pounced on top of her like a leopard.

Chapter Eight

SALMON CROQUETTES SIZZLED IN OLIVE oil inside the hot frying pan on top of the stove. Beside the stove on the counter, the Keurig hummed, brewing a small cup of raspberry tea. Sandella inhaled the mixed aromas, sliced a tablespoon of butter into the simmering grits, added a dash of salt, and then stirred.

As the meal settled into its last stages of cooking, she walked over to the window. She slid her hands inside her apron. Two birds perched on the branch of her favorite oak. They began pecking each other beaks.

Ahh, they're in love. Like me. Last night after they'd made love, she'd left the cottage and come back to the main house. Just as she'd crawled into bed, Braylon emerged in the doorway and ended up joining her. They'd made love three times last night and eventually she'd fallen asleep with him holding her.

Braylon had no clue how deeply and madly in love she was with him. It'd been on the tip of her tongue to tell him last night after they'd made mad passionate love the last time. But she couldn't. She didn't believe in women announcing their undying love for a man first. It just wasn't right.

For all she knew he might never love her and might very well end things once Willa and Drake returned. Who knew? As charming and as handsome as he was, she was certain the women on the base would eventually make a move, if they hadn't done so already.

Lord help me. He'd captured her heart like no man ever had. Having sex *before* knowing where the relationship was headed... why in the world did she let this happen?

"It smells delicious in here." Braylon startled the heck out of her.

She turned around sharply. "Good morning."

"You're up and going early, but then again, you're always are. A hardworking woman is tough to find these days, especially one that's genuine."

So are you saying that I'm your woman? Darn it. Why didn't she have the nerve to ask the questions she deserved to know the answers to? Like...where did she stand with him? "That's what I hear. Would you like some breakfast?"

He looked at the time on his watch. "Normally I don't eat a heavy breakfast, but this smells too good to turn down. And I love salmon croquettes."

Just as she pulled a plate down from the cupboard the phone rang. She hefted it from its base and dropped it to her ear. "Hello."

"Sandella, darling. Good morning." It was Willa.

She placed a hand over the mouthpiece and softly whispered, "It's your grandmother."

Braylon smiled, then nodded. "Oh."

"How's everything going, darling?" she asked, in her usual southern, sophisticated drawl.

"Everything's fine. I picked Royce up from Gladys's yesterday, and he's so happy to be home."

Braylon pressed his chest up against her breasts, cupped her butt, and nibbled the crook of her neck. Chills engulfed her. *Oh God, not while I'm on the phone.*

"Yes, he's more comfortable at home. How's your health doing?"

Braylon hiked the apron to her hips, smashed his erection up against her stomach, and slid his hands down her jeans straight into her core. When he slid his tongue inside her free ear, her knees buckled.

Her eyes closed halfway. Bucking against his probing fingers, she palmed his shoulder to steady herself against his hard physique. Licking her parched lips, her breath hitched. It was a darn shame she exuded no control in another woman's kitchen.

"I asked, how's your health?" Willa's voice snapped her from her trance.

"It's good. Real good," she said, referring to Braylon's enticing ministrations more so than her well-being.

"How's that grandson of mine treating you?"

"Oh Willa," she purred. She removed his hand from her sex so she could think better, then covered the mouthpiece of the phone. "Stop it," she mouthed, playfully hitting the back of his hand. He burst into loud laughter then went over to the sink to wash his hands.

"Sandella, is that grandson of mine bothering you? I mean, I heard him laugh, and you seem mighty distracted."

"No. He's not bothering me." *At least not like you think he is.*

"Then what has him so tickled this early in the morning?"

"It must be something he's reading in the paper," she fibbed.

Braylon curled his fingers into a circle, then flicked his tongue through the hole as if he was eating her pussy. Her mouth dropped open. He stood over the stove cracking up.

"All righty then...well, Drake and I should be back any day

now. As I'm sure you already know, his mother hasn't died yet. The woman is one helluva good faker. But anyhow, if you start feeling ill or need anything, don't hesitate to give me a call."

"Thanks, Willa."

"No, thank you, Sandella. I appreciate everything you do for me and my son. Tell Braylon I'll see him soon." She ended the call.

She placed the phone back on the receiver. "I can't believe you!"

Braylon gave her a lusty grin. "Yes, you can. And you liked every bit of it, too." His cell vibrated against his hip. He pulled the cell out of his clip and spied the caller ID. "It's my brother, Sonny. Wonder why he's calling so early in the morning." He hit the button on the screen. "Hello."

Payback is hell. While Braylon stood talking on the phone with his brother, Sandella reached inside his pants and pulled out his cock. At the sight of his heavy veinedshaft, her mouth watered.

She dropped to her knees, wrapped her fingers around his shaft, then lusciously curled her mouth around his swollen head. As she pressed her lips down his thick length, his eyes became huge and disbelieving.

Wagging a finger at her, he swallowed. "I…I…will," he stuttered, incompetent to finish his sentence. He moaned and the deep noise made him sound like he was strangling. Without saying goodbye, he tapped the screen, then placed the phone on the counter.

"Now this is just wrong." He palmed the back of her head.

"Mmmm, hmmm." She hummed on his pulsating member. Sausage for breakfast had never tasted better, Sandella thought, her head bobbing up and down.

BRAYLON'S FEET DAMN NEAR SHUFFLED as he walked hurriedly inside his office, his keys jingling deep inside his pants pocket. He flicked on the lights, locked the door behind himself, hastened behind his desk, then plopped down in his chair. Never in his life had he been this slow when getting to work. Taking another shower after the hot sex he'd engaged in with Sandella had resulted in this.

The time on his desk flashed to 7:49 as he sought to catch his breath. Damn, he was only eleven minutes early, he thought, berating himself for succumbing to Sandella before leaving the house. But then again, there wasn't a man on this earth who would've been stupid enough to refuse such advances.

He hit the power button on his computer thinking he had to get to work at least thirty minutes early from now on. Fooling around with Sandella this morning had had him rushing to the office again today. She'd sucked him like a pro. Waking up to a good breakfast and a mind-boggling blow job was something he could get used to. If the two of them ever got married, he'd have to buy them a house close to the base. *Jesus, why does the word* married *keep popping up in my head?*

Focus. Focus. He shook his head. He reached inside his desk, pulled out Sugar's file, and spread it open on his desk. After Sandella had fallen asleep last night, he'd opened his work laptop, pulled up the criminal database, and had found out the name of the guy that'd been found murdered in the woods. The guy's name was Marc Jackson.

He entered Marc Jackson's name in the search box to read over the case that'd been long ago forgotten, again. A picture of the blond-haired white man with light green eyes posted to the top right hand corner. He clicked to the number two at the bottom on the page.

"Now that's interesting," Braylon said. The thick-browed Forest Greene had handled Marc Jackson's case. His boss's boss, Forest, had concluded in the report that Marc Jackson had been shot by a hunter. However, there was no substantial evidence supporting the conclusion.

"Morning, Detective!"

Braylon's head snapped up from the screen. Forest's head inched between the space of the door and the frame. A wicked smile lifted his wide-spread lips. *Never mind knocking.* "Good morning."

An evil light sparked the man's green eyes. "I see you barely got here on time again today," he remarked.

Yeah, I was getting my cock sucked. Because Forest's condescension irked him, he turned the table. "Let me ask you something."

"Shoot," Forest said, coming to stand fully in his office.

Braylon observed the man's face. "What do you know about Private Marc Jackson's death?"

Forest's thick brows scrunched. As his eyes darkened to the color of split pea soup, his full lips thinned into a straight line. Irritation was written on his face like red ink on white paper. "I know a lot, Wexler. In fact I was the one who handled the damn case. What's with all the questions?"

Braylon tried to give the man a sincere look. "A good friend of mine happened to mention how much he missed him while shooting a game of pool the other night. So it got me to thinking about him, that's all."

Forest fought hard to hide his frustration, but Braylon could see straight through the man. "Oh. Well, that case was closed a long time ago. And if I were you, I'd be careful who I ask about him."

"Why's that?"

"Because the last person that did, ended up regretting it." Forest turned on heels, and as he walked toward the door, his hands balled into tight fists.

You're hiding something, Forest. And I'm going to find out what it is.

LATE IN THE AFTERNOON, BRAYLON aimed for the toilet water as he stood pissing at the urinal. Today had been an informative day. Because he'd received training before his arrival, he was able to get better acquainted with personnel as well as his surroundings.

He'd had the privilege of running into Alyssa while out on the lawn making small talk with some of the officers. She'd had the audacity to follow him inside the office and flirt unrelentingly until he'd entered the bathroom. The big-breasted girl had no qualms about making her desires for him known either. And she—

"Unnhhk," the voice resounded in the stall behind him, sounding as if he was taking a dump. Braylon hurried to zip his grey trousers. He turned toward the noise. The person inside the stall let out a bomb of a fart. "Excuse me, Wexler," Forest grunted, "but those damn collards they served for lunch got me to shitting like a bull."

There wasn't a damn thing tactful about Forest. "I'm glad I didn't have any."

Fart. Fart. "Yep. I wish I would've had a bowl of chicken soup instead."

A grave stench wafted up Braylon's nose, he practically jogged out of the bathroom. How Forest ever make it up the ranks was beyond Braylon. The man had an infuriating attitude. And he was unpleasant to say the least. According to the men and women on the base earlier, many of them feared him. But they never said why.

After Braylon retrieved his mail, he stalked into his office and took a seat. Needing to mask his pesto chicken panini breath, he opened his desk drawer, popped a piece of Dentyne gum into his mouth, then opened the brown envelope with *confidential* stamped in red on it.

What the hell? A green index card with a typewritten message lay inside. He brought the note up to his eyes.

Dear Detective Wexler,

Solve the end of this riddle and it'll direct you to Sugar's killer. Please be careful.

Your boy, Simon.

The bush of his brows is downright scary.

Not because of the shape, but because they so damn hairy.

A pit bull ain't got nothing on him.

He's tall.

He's mean.

His last name is—

Braylon's heart dunked. "Fucking Greene." Like the last envelope, this one didn't have a return address. This Simon character's determination to keep a low profile gave him the creeps. He didn't know who to trust. Well, he knew he definitely didn't trust Forest, but thing was, he didn't trust this Simon guy either. For all he knew, Simon wasn't even his real name.

Tension rose from the pit of his stomach and shocked the sides of his brain. Reclining in his chair, he rubbed at the sides of his bulging, throbbing temples. It was hard to think with such intense, riveting pain.

If Simon wants justice why doesn't he come forward? He said he can't. They'll kill him. Who are they? Forest and who else?

He wrapped up some loose ends, shut down his laptop, jumped to his feet and headed for outdoors. He hopped inside his Hummer, slammed the door, and drove off. What would Marc Jackson's wife, Theresa, have to say about her husband's death? he wondered, driving past the guard's station and pulling out onto the road.

"WHO IS IT?" A CHILD'S voice rang out on the other side of the door from where Braylon stood.

"It's Detective Braylon Wexler. Is your mother home?"

"Mooooom!" the young boy yelled out loud. "Some man with big muscles is here to see you!"

"Yes." The woman said behind the closed door.

"My name is Braylon Wexler." He held up his shield. "I'm an investigator for the Marines. If you don't mind, I'd like to speak with you about your late husband, Marc."

The door opened to a beautiful African-American woman, with shoulder length hair. She stood under a gleaming light bulb. "What did you say your name was?" she asked, blinking her eyes.

"Detective Braylon Wexler."

She grasped her chest. "Please tell me they *finally* arrested my husband's killer."

"No ma'am, we haven't. But if you're not busy, I'd like to ask you a few questions."

"Come in." She stepped to the side and held the door open for him.

Braylon strode past her into the living room. The aroma of fried chicken crept inside his nose. "Something smells delicious."

"Thanks. I just finished cooking fried chicken, corn bread, and collard greens."

At the mention of collard greens his stomach turned. Forest had said earlier that the greens had made his bowels loose, and he'd stunk up the entire bathroom at work. His crap had smelled worse than the dead bodies in Iraq. "Mrs. Jackson."

"Theresa."

"Okay. Theresa."

She gestured toward the sofa. "Please sit."

"Thanks." As he took a seat on the grey couch in front of the window, she sat across from him on the loveseat.

"They killed Marc, you know?"

That's the same thing Simon says. Braylon reached into the pocket of his shirt and pulled out a pad with a new, black leather cover. "What makes you say that?"

"Because Marc told me that they were going to kill him."

"Who are they?"

A tight ball was visible in her throat. "I don't know any names. But Marc told me," her voice cracked, "he was getting threatening letters at work. And a few times he received threats on his cell phone."

"Did he report this to law enforcement?"

"Yes."

"To who?"

"Detective Forest Greene." She folded her arms over her chest. "That mean bastard just turned his head and looked the other way. As a matter of fact, he never bothered to return any of my phone calls. And every time I tried to see him, he downright dismissed my numerous requests."

Braylon wrote down each word she said. Gripping the black ink pen, he lifted his eyes from the paper. "Did you tell Detective Greene of your suspicions?"

She shook her head. "Not verbally, but I did write a letter to him."

Hmmm. Her letter wasn't in the file. "What did the letter say?"

She released a heavy breath. Her shoulders sagged. "In short, it said that I suspected someone on the base had killed Marc."

"Theresa. Why did Marc think someone was trying to kill him?"

"He'd overheard someone bragging about how they'd raped and killed Sugar Summers. Did you know her?"

"No."

"Oh."

"Did Marc give you a name of the person bragging?"

"Yes."

"Who?"

"Spencer Knox."

Braylon's stomach churned violently as if he'd eaten some spoiled collards like that killer Forest had earlier. *Both Forest and Spencer may be Sugar's killers.*

His gut tightened and rolled into a big knot.

Chapter Nine

AROUND EIGHT O'CLOCK IN THE evening Braylon sat at the kitchen table. Gritting his teeth, he swiped a heavy hand down his face. The information Theresa had given him pertaining to her deceased husband Marc made for incriminating evidence against his superiors. Because it was his job to protect the Marines on the base as well as the people in the community, he had no choice but to fulfill his duties by seeking justice.

I'm on to you, Forest and Spencer. Fist to chin and musing over his next move, he heard Sandella's car. Seeing her was going to be like a breath of fresh air.

Drayton and the upcoming paternity test quickly entered his mind. A part of him felt as if he was betraying Sandella by keeping this a secret from her. However, being forthcoming wasn't necessarily the right thing to do either. Madison sure had put him in an awful dilemma that could very well cause him to lose the best thing that had ever happened to him—Sandella. *If Drayton's mine, I will not leave him like my father left me.*

Sandella entered from the back door off the garage toting an armful of plastic grocery bags. Royce was on her heels carrying a bag in each hand, too. As soon as her gaze connected with his she bedazzled him with a sexy smile. "Hi."

"Let me get that for you," Braylon said, quickening to her side. He hurried to take the bags from her steely grip.

"Thanks."

He placed the bags on the counter. "How was your day?"

"It was good. Yours?" she asked, digging inside one of the bags and pulling out a fresh bunch of broccoli.

He didn't dare tell her some guy named Simon had put him in a most dangerous situation involving her mother. She'd have a fit if she knew her mother's case had been reopened, and he didn't bother telling her about it. "Busy." He offered her the simplest answer.

She turned the knob on the stove to high. "How does baked barbeque chicken, broccoli, and cheesy scalloped potatoes sound for dinner?"

Braylon turned the stove back off. "It sounds good, but you're not cooking tonight."

"I'm not?"

"Nope. Running SugarKanes, taking care of Royce, your father, and Drew...I think you need to take some time off to relax."

She giggled. "You sound like my father. He often says the same thing."

Other than his mother, he'd never seen a woman work as hard as she did. "He's right." His eyes traveled to the brown bag sitting on the counter behind him. He reached inside and slid out a foil baking dish. "I picked up some baked ziti and a bottle of wine from Villa Castiano."

"Mmm. I love Villa Castiano. Their garlic rolls are to die for."

"I thought maybe we could take a boat ride across the river and have dinner."

Her eyes beamed. "I'd love that. I've never been on Drake's boat before. I'm going to go grab a sweater for Royce."

"He's not going."

"Say what? Well, who's going to keep—"

"I am," Adam emerged from the family room.

"Adam! When did you get back?" Her heart lit up.

The salt-and-pepper haired man smiled. "About two hours ago."

"How was your vacation in New York?" She sounded amused.

"Terrific. But it feels good to be back on the island. At this old age, the big city life isn't for me anymore. The hectic traffic alone makes me tired and gives me migraines." He chuckled.

"Are you sure you don't mind watching Royce?"

"I'm positive. We're going to play memory match and watch a movie on DVD."

"Let's get a move on." Braylon hefted the baking dish while Sandella gathered the brown bag containing the rolls and eating utensils.

The cool night air smoothed over him as they walked along the dock. Glowing, Sandella kept in stride beside him. He stepped onto Drake's luxurious, Sea Ray Sundancer boat, rounded the corner, then dipped his head to descend the steps to the level beneath.

Equipped with fine, white leather sofas, the spacious area below included a bathroom, a kitchen filled with stainless steel appliances, and a nice big circular bed. A white furry animal throw was strewn across the light blue comforter.

Sandella lowered the bag to the counter then put her hands on her hips. She looked around the lavish room. "I'm assuming you know how to drive a boat?"

He popped the bottle of Zinfandel into the refrigerator. "And a motorcycle, and a jet ski, and *you.*"

"Me?"

"Yes, you." He put his mouth on hers. "I plan to drive you mad tonight in this bed, woman."

"Oh my," were the only words that'd come from her succulent lips.

As Braylon sailed across the rippling waves of the river, bright lights emanating from the hull cast down on the black water. The blue moon above shadowed them. Sandella sat next to him.

Her legs were crossed at the knees, her fingers were steepled in her lap, and strands of hair blew across her beautiful face. Being here like this with her made him feel complete.

It'd been weeks now since he'd first bedded her. Yet still, he was just as interested in spending time with her today as he'd been upon first meeting her. He'd never been this way with any other woman. Guess there was a first time for everything.

Reaching the other side of the river some fifteen minutes later, he steered the boat toward the dock behind a huge white mansion and parked. After he anchored the boat, he stepped onto the dock, then reached for her hand and pulled her to him.

"Where are we?"

"Harbor Island."

"A lot of rich people live out this way."

"Yes. You're right."

Braylon stepped down onto the flat land. Returning to face her, he extended his arms for her. She hooked an arm around his neck. He captured her into his embrace. "I can walk."

"I know, but I like holding you." Carrying her across the wet grass, he pecked her lips, then finally lowered her to her feet.

Colonial columns encircled the back porch of the white two-story building in front of them. A steeply pitched roof irregular shape and covered in textured shingles graced the top. A full-length, asymmetrical porch wrapped around the entire house.

"Wow, this is beautiful."

His gaze clung to the sign under the oak. He pointed to the sign posted under the tree. "It's for sale, too."

"I'll never own a house like this."

"Never say never."

"Working as a caretaker, I think saying never is realistic."

But if I make you my wife, you wouldn't have to ever work another day in your life. "Let's walk along the boardwalk." Braylon slipped his hand around hers.

Suddenly, an older gentleman emerged on the rear porch. He waved. "Howdy!"

Braylon waved in return. "Nice house."

"I saw you looking at it. Are you interested in buying it?"

"As a matter of fact I am."

Sandella nudged his side.

"Then why don't you come and take a look around?"

"Don't mind if I do."

Braylon and Sandella walked hand in hand toward the house. "I can't believe you," she said through clenched teeth.

"You never know. If the price is right, I may buy this instead of a condo."

"Really?"

"Really."

When the kindhearted gentleman, who said his name was Clyde Basil Parker, opened the door, Braylon inhaled the sweet scent of spicy cranberry. "My wife and I were sitting here by the window drinking hot cranberry tea when the two of you came up. We were youngsters just like the two of you when we got married and moved into this house. How long y'all been married?"

"We're not married," Sandella said.

The man gave Braylon a look of utter disbelief. With his pants coming up past his navel, he stopped in his tracks. He pulled his glasses from the pocket of his pants that rested higher than his navel, slid the glasses up the bridge of his nose, then pinned Sandella with a scrutinizing stare. "Not marrying a pretty sweet thing like her," his eyes scrolled over her body, "you must be a risk taker, or just plain old foolish," he told Braylon. The man snatched off his glasses. "Do you need to borrow these so you can see what I'm talking about?" He let loose a wet sounding laugh.

Braylon chuckled. He draped an arm around her neck. "No thanks, sir. I may be a lot of things, but foolish ain't one of them. I know I have a good thing." He squeezed her shoulder for emphasis.

SANDELLA'S CHEEKS BURNED. STANDING IN the stranger's family room she wondered if Braylon was trying to impress the man or if he was serious when he'd implied she was his. Hoping it was the later, she mounted the steps to the top of the staircase. The home she was touring captivated her. It was fit for a princess.

The man handed Braylon a card. "Just call my realtor if you decide you'd like to buy it."

"Will do. Nice meeting you, Buddy."

"I think you should buy it for that gal of yours. Oh yeah, rumor has it this house brings couples the best of luck and lots of babies."

The thought of having lots of babies with Braylon warmed her as they sailed further down the river. Short minutes later, he steered the boat up to a public docking area and parked. If she didn't know any better, she'd think Braylon had planned the visit to the stranger's house. But if that were the case, why wouldn't he have told her? Could it be he was planning to pop the question, marry her, then buy her that house? *Aw shucks,* she was getting in way over her head.

After she warmed their food, they had the pleasure of sitting at the table, devouring pasta smothered in spicy tomato sauce, covered with sharp parmesan cheese.

Braylon tossed their paper plates in the trash. "How about roasted marshmallows for dessert?" he asked, holding up a bag.

Giddy, she clapped her hands in front of her face like a little kid. "Where are we going to roast them?"

"Outdoors. Come."

Braylon found a nice spot not far from the covered area with picnic tables to enjoy their dessert. Sandella spread a rugged blue blanket on the grass. Free of bugs and humidity, the cool night was perfect for roasting a tasty dessert. She sat.

He reached into the tree above his head for a twig, popped it, then rubbed the halves together starting a fire. "What are you thinking about?"

She bent her legs at the knees and looked up at him. "I'm thinking how talented you are to have started a fire like that."

"No biggy. Marines are taught many things for survival."

Smiling, "Well, I'm impressed." *There's nothing like a manly man. So strong. So dominating. And smart.*

As they sat dangling the melting treats over the fire the sweet aroma permeated her nose. He turned his eyes to capture her gaze, then smiled. She felt herself melting worse than the candy under his drugging trance.

After the marshmallow cooled, he slid it from the stick and fed it to her. Her jaws sucked inwardly as she wrapped her tongue around his finger. Excitement flickered in his eyes. Before she had time to swallow it all the way, he slanted his mouth over hers and kissed her. As their tongues mated some of the sweet treat slithered from her mouth into his. Groaning, he swallowed it all.

Heat pounded inside her center. Her walls clenched. She wanted him inside her so badly that her entrance ached.

He slid his hand into the top of her dress, pulled out her breast, then plopped the tight nipple in his mouth. "We can't do it out here," she protested, looking around to find they were all alone, surrounded in darkness.

"Yes we can. And we are." He mouthed her swollen flesh.

I don't think I can resist him. Only teenagers did things this risky and inappropriate, she thought, knowing it was only a matter of time before she gave into his strong advances. Unable to stop the madness, she clamped her hands onto his shoulder. Her head lolled backward. Her chest heaved. Her breath came out in short wisps. "What if we get caught?" she asked, her eyes soaking up the sight of the full blue moon. *This man is a beast.*

His hands ruffled against her back. "We won't. Hop on."

Her gaze fell to his lap to find his bare erection sticking straight up. She licked her lips then eased over into his lap, putting her back to his chest. While on her knees she hiked up her dress.

With a firm hand on the lower part of her spine, he inserted into her from behind, filling her to the hilt. When she fell down into his lap his shaft seemed to go past her navel. Her stomach felt full.

As she rode him backward he reached around and pinched her nipples. Her whimpering sounds sounded like a small puppy. He felt so good inside her. *I can't believe I'm doing this.* Circling her hips, she nibbled her bottom lip. She was more certain now than ever that Braylon had her under his spell and there was no turning back, at least not for her.

THE CONSTANT SOUND OF THE cell buzzing on the nightstand persuaded Braylon to open his eyes. *What time is it?* The bright red numbers of the alarm clock emblazoned 1:38 a.m. With Sandella spooned up against him, he reached over to answer the phone. "Hello," he said groggily, his eyes blinking in the darkness. *It better not be Madison.*

"They burned down my house!" a woman bellowed in his ears,

then followed up with a screeching cry.

Braylon detached Sandella's hands from his chest and bolted upright. The raspy voice sounded familiar. "Mrs. Jackson. Is that you?"

Sniffling. Crying. "Yes."

"What happened?"

"Somebody set the house on fire while I was asleep. If it hadn't been for my neighbor banging on my bedroom window, I would've died! I think this has to do with your visit earlier. They're going to kill me!"

Sandella eased up in bed. "Is everything okay?" she asked, pulling the string on the lamp. The room brightened.

Holding up a finger, Braylon shook his head. "Where are you now?"

"I'm across the street at my neighbor's house."

"I'm on my way." He ended the call, jumped to his feet, shrugged on his shirt, then quickly yanked his jeans over his hips.

A wary expression developed on Sandella's face. "Where are you going?" she asked, standing.

"A work emergency has come up."

"This time of night?"

"Detectives are on call twenty-four seven." There was no doubt in his mind that Theresa Jackson's home had been purposely set on fire, which meant someone had followed him to her home earlier and had felt the need to silence her...for good. "Sorry for waking you."

"You didn't wake me. I was about to get up to use the bathroom anyway."

He grabbed his Beretta. *Click. Click.* He slid back the magazine. After counting the ammunition, he slid the heavy piece into the holster looped tightly around his waist.

Pop! Pop! Gunfire crackled the air then shots rained through the window.

His heart caved. "Get down!" He shoved Sandella, causing her to fall to the floor flat on her face with a resounding clunk. He clicked off the light.

"Is that gunfire?" On her hands and knees she scrambled away from the window to the other side of the bed.

"Yes. Stay down." Using extreme caution, he kept his back pinned to the wall as he made his way to the side of the window. He pushed a small corner of the fabric from the shattered glass of the window to spy outside, and caught the taillights of a car. Screeching tires pierced the air as the car sped off. *Damn, they're getting away.*

"Get dressed and get Royce dressed too," he demanded, blood boiling in his veins. "Leave the lights off."

"I'm afraid." Sandella stood shaking next to the closet.

He wrapped his hands around her shivering body, hoping to calm her. "I know you're scared, baby," he quickly pecked her forehead, "but I'm not going to let anyone hurt you." He could deal with the bastard trying to bring harm to him. But putting Sandella's and Royce's lives at stake? They were going to pay for such stupidity. *I'm going to kill the bastard who did this.* He made a promise to himself. *Fucking coward.*

Chapter Ten

"OH GOD, BRAYLON. WHY DIDN'T you tell me this before now?" Sandella sat in the passenger seat of the car stunned that Braylon had reopened her mother's case.

"I didn't want you to worry."

"I appreciate your concern." She sighed. "This is what my family and I have been praying for."

He grunted. "I'm going to find the man that killed your mother and put your life in danger tonight."

"Thanks." As she caressed the back of his hand, the dark look of anger dulling his eyes worried her.

Now on the other side of town in Beaufort, after descending the bridge, he turned right at the corner. "Maybe worry is not the right word. I just thought it'd be best if you didn't know so you could stay focused on running SugarKanes and taking care of Royce."

"I still wish you'd told me, but I do understand. My dad can never know about this until after the fact. If he knew he'd try to play detective and put himself in danger."

"The less people who know, including your father, the better."

When they reached Theresa's street, the potent scent of burning wood engulfed her. Taking in the sight of the red and blue lights flashing over the area, she felt the car coming to a slow stop. A cop started toward them, and Braylon reached for his shield.

The middle-aged officer signaled him to roll down his window. He hit the button and the glass lowered. The officer cleared his throat. "There's been a fire. Turn around and take the alternate route."

His badge had been there for the officer to see, but apparently he'd overlooked it. "I'm with CID," he said, bringing the shield up to the man's eye level.

I can't believe he's reinvestigating my mother's death. Aric, Chandler, and Drew would be so happy if they knew. But I'm not telling them until it's all over.

Braylon parked on the curb a few houses down from the fire. Lacing her fingers in her lap, Sandella shifted her gaze to the windshield. Theresa emerged from her neighbor's front door. A few seconds later so did Sandella's father.

Dread gripped her. "Dear...Lord." *What's he doing here?*

Braylon was about to get out of the car but stopped short. "What?"

She swallowed the fear. When Theresa pointed toward the Hummer, her father's head snapped in their direction. "See that man in the wheelchair next to Theresa?"

"Yes. He's pointing at us."

Her breathing seemed halted. "That's my father. I bet he knows."

"Knows what?"

"That I'm dating a Marine." *This night just keeps getting uglier.*

"It's going to be fine, Sandella. I'll handle your father."

No one handles Kane.

Kane's resolute gaze was fixed on the Hummer as he wheeled himself toward them. The closer he got, the harder her heart thrummed. He stopped when he reached the driver's side door. Fire burned in his dark eyes. "Get out so we can talk like two grown men!"

"Don't come out until I've had a chance to speak with him," Braylon warned Sandella. He stepped out the Hummer into the thick smoky air.

Kane's cold dark eyes surveyed Braylon like a wild animal about to tackle his prey. "Are you Braylon Wexler?"

"Yes sir. I am."

Frowning and glaring up at Braylon, Kane bared his teeth. His hands curled around the arms of the wheelchair. "I don't care who you are, Detective. No daughter of mine is dating a Marine. Do I make myself clear?" Giving orders to a lawman, apparently her father had lost his mind.

"Yes, you do, sir. I'll promise to leave your daughter alone, but only under one condition." He pushed his hands into his pockets.

Kane gritted his teeth. "Sandy is not up for negotiation."

Sandella came and stood next to her father. She placed a hand on his shoulder. "Will you just please hear him out?" she asked, praying that Braylon could talk some sense into her old man.

"Let me try and calm my damn nerves first." Kane lit a cigarette. Smoke spiraled from his full lips. "This better be good."

Braylon glared down at Kane. "I'll give you my word to leave Sandella alone for now."

Sandella's heart ping-ponged in her chest at his surprising words.

Coughing, Kane's brows shot up. "For now?"

"I'll leave her alone for now...*if* you promise...to give us your blessing to continue our relationship *after* I find your wife's killer."

Tears wet Kane's eyes. A muscle flickered in his jaw. "That case was closed a long time ago."

"It's been reopened."

"By who?"

"Me."

Kane pulled his misty gaze away to think. Nodding, he returned his focus back to Braylon. He blew out a ragged smoky breath. "I feel like I'm making a deal with the devil to save my own soul."

Sandella stooped in front of her father's chair to look into his eyes, caressing her hands over his. "He's not the devil, Daddy. He's a great man, with a good heart," she choked out.

"So do we have a deal?" Braylon extended his hand to Kane.

"If you find my wife's killer," a tear rolled down his cheek, "I'll give you two my blessing." He shook Braylon's hand. "Now let's go, Sandy."

To keep peace, Sandella decided it'd be best for her and Royce to leave as her father had instructed.

BRAYLON STOOD AT THE REAR of the truck watching Sandella disappear beyond the cloud of smoke filtering the air. Walking beside her father, she clasped Royce's hand, then glanced back over her shoulder at him. She mouthed, "Thanks."

It broke Braylon's heart to turn away from her. As he strode across the lawn toward Theresa he thought of how she didn't need to thank him for being respectful toward her father. He'd been raised to respect his elders. Never in a million years would he drive a wedge between a father and his daughter by continuing to date her without the man's blessing. As precious as his Sandella was, she deserved a man who was willing to earn her father's respect. And bring union to her family, not division.

I don't care if it takes me forever. I'm going to bring Sandella and her family peace.

"How are you holding up?" Braylon asked Theresa.

"I'm terrified, Detective." Her fearful eyes scanned over the perimeter. "Somebody wants me dead."

"You're not safe here. Do you have a family member out of town you can stay with until this is over?"

She nodded. "Yes. But I'm not running away, I'm staying right here. I am going to send my son to live with his aunt, though."

Wanting to shake some sense into the stubborn lady, he ground his molars instead. "Theresa. You don't know who you're dealing with. Whoever killed Sugar and Marc wants you dead too. And they won't stop until they succeed. You need to leave Beaufort tonight, definitely no later than tomorrow morning."

Theresa folded her arms under her breasts. Just as she parted her mouth to speak, a detective walked up to her. "Mrs. Jackson. Do you know anyone by the name of Simon?"

Simon? Braylon's ears perked up.

Shaking her head, she said, "No. Why?"

"Because someone by the name of Simon dispatched 911 right before your house caught on fire to report a man lurking around your bedroom window."

Shaking her head, Theresa clenched her chest. "I don't know anyone by the name of Simon."

Braylon asked, "Did this Simon guy get a description of the man or his car tag number?"

The detective shook his head. "Unfortunately, Simon stated there wasn't a tag on the car. As far as a description of the man, the only thing Simon told dispatch was that he thought the perpetrator had worn all black. It was too dark to see anything."

Fear was evident in Theresa's shaky voice. "Why didn't this Simon guy just stay and talk with the police? What was he doing here in the first place?"

"That's what we're trying to figure out."

Braylon said, "We'll do our best to find Simon and the person that destroyed your home."

"I still can't believe this is happening," was all she had to say.

AT THE FIRST SIGN OF daylight, Sandella rolled out of bed at her father's house and dragged herself to the bathroom across the hallway. She'd tossed and turned throughout the entire night and now fatigue threatened to zap the little strength she did have. She washed her hands and lathered her toothbrush with toothpaste.

The bristles of the electric toothbrush rotated over her teeth. *Royce hates it here. He kept me and Dad up all night asking to go home.* She gargled the minty flavored mouthwash.

Although she knew he disliked it there, she had no choice but to bring him home with her, especially after everything that had occurred last night. Not only had someone put her life in jeopardy, but Braylon had promised her father that he'd leave her alone until he found her mother's killer. How likely was he to keep his promise? Better yet, would she be able to keep her hands off him? Already she missed him. Missed his big arms around her... missed his manly lips kissing her...missed his tongue flicking over her nipples. Her body tingled from the sensual thoughts.

"This is not going to work," she said quietly, making her way down the hallway. When she reached the living room and spotted her father sleeping by the window with a rifle across his lap, sadness mixed with pride touched her heart. With his head bowed, he was snoring like a grizzly bear. Knowing him, he'd stayed up guarding the house all night, and hadn't fallen asleep until just recently.

"Dad," she called.

Kane's body jerked awake swiftly. "Huh?" Bewilderment settled on his face. His eyes were puffy and red like he'd cried off and on throughout the night.

Sandella put a hand on his shoulder. "Why don't you go to bed and lie down?"

Grief clouded his black eyes. "Do you really think that detective friend of yours can help us?"

She shrugged. "I don't know for sure, Dad, but I do know that Braylon will do his best and try."

Still grieving his wife, her father was desperate for justice to come to his family and so was she. He nodded. His lips trembled as if the horrible memories of her death were still haunting him. "We begged them damn fools, the damn police to help us, and they just ignored the shit out of us. It's about goddamn time somebody did something sensible on our behalf. "That friend of yours…" his voice trailed off.

"What about Braylon?"

"I saw it in his eyes."

"You saw what, Dad?"

"Trust. Sincerity. He's gone find the son of a bitch that killed my Sugar. I saw pure determination in his eyes."

"I hope you're right."

"Me too." He yawned. "I'm going to go and get some sl—"

Suddenly, the door cracked open. Kane cocked his weapon and aimed it at the door. "Get in the back, Sandy," he grumbled.

"Dad! Sandy!" Sandella's brother called out. "It's me, Aric."

"Damn, boy, why you ain't call before bursting in here like a robber?" Kane lowered his weapon.

Aric emerged inside the living room wearing a pair of blue jeans and a red sweater. Usually he'd smile when seeing them, but today his lips settled in a thin line. He threw his arms around his baby sister and squeezed her tight. "I did try calling, but the line was busy."

Kane shook his head. "Royce kept talking on the phone last night and done went and left it off the hook."

Sandella smiled. "He was probably trying to call Willa to come get him. Right after I make breakfast, I'm going to head over to the island."

"Are you okay?" Aric quizzed, giving her an endearing stare.

She put her hand over her heart. "I'm fine. You didn't have to come all this way to see about me——"

"Yes, he did. And I did, too." Chandler came through the door with a huge smile on his face. He dropped the black suitcase to the floor and spread his arms open for her.

"Chandler!" Sandella shouted, running up to him and throwing her arms around his waist. "You guys are too much," her voice pitched as she nuzzled her head against Chandler's chest.

Wearing a long-sleeve, navy cotton shirt with matching bottoms, Drew emerged from the hallway yawning and rubbing a knuckle over his eyeball. "Next time y'all need to come after noon. A brotha is trying to get his rest so he can be ready for the ladies."

"Be quiet, big head." Aric gave Drew a bear hug.

With one hand wrapped around Sandella, Chandler held out his fist to Drew. "How about some football later?"

"I'm down with that," Drew said, bumping his fist.

"Home. Home," Royce said, coming out of the kitchen, walking up to Sandella.

She caressed his arm. "Okay, Royce. I'll take you home. Give me a second to get dressed. Okay?"

His face split into a handsome smile. "K."

Aric's brows set in a straight line. "Do the police have any leads or idea who was trying to kill you last night?"

"Not yet. At least not that I'm aware of."

Kane cleared his throat. "Should I tell her or you?"

"What?"

Aric's face was serious, his lips set in a straight line. "We came here to get you and take you back to DC with us."

Sandella placed her hands on her hips. "DC? Get me? What do you mean?"

Chandler cupped her shoulders. "Look, Sandy. We're not about to let the same thing that happened to Mom happen to you. You're coming home with us."

"I'm not leaving here to go to DC."

Chandler frowned. "Yes, you are...even if I have to drag you out of here. You're going."

"I can't leave even if I wanted too."

"Why not?" The brothers asked simultaneously.

"Well, I was going to wait to announce it, but I guess now is as good as ever."

Kane rolled his eyes. "Lord Jesus. If this here girl says she's getting married, I'm gone stroke right on outta here."

Sandella laughed. "Dad, you're so funny. I'm not getting married." *I wish.* "But I can't go because I started a bakery business...SugarKanes."

Kane's eyes widened. "What's the name of the bakery again?"

She smiled. "SugarKanes."

"You have a bakery named after me and your mother?

"Yes."

"Oh, Sandy. This just melts my heart."

"SugarKanes sells assorted desserts, but our specialty is my caramel pecan pies. I'm meeting with a realtor next week to discuss renting out some space near the island. And if business keeps booming like it presently is, I'm going to open up a bakery right here in Beaufort, too."

Tears settled on Kane's lashes. "SugarKanes? I'm so glad you named it after me and your mother. I'm so proud of you."

"Yes. But I can't take all the credit. Braylon thought of the name for me," she admitted, bashfully. "He even helped me set up my online bakery, distribution and all. If it weren't for him,

SugarKanes wouldn't be happening."

Kane sniffed. His gaze dropped to his lap. He slowly lifted his head. "Just go ahead."

"Go ahead? Huh?" she said.

"You have my blessing to date the damn man," Kane growled.

"You're giving her your blessing to date a—"

"Marine!" all three brothers shouted in unison.

Sandella's lips curved into a big grateful smile. She eased into her father's lap, wrapped her arms around his neck, and nuzzled her forehead against his. "Thanks, Dad."

Chapter Eleven

THE TORTUROUS EVENTS THAT'D OCCURRED last night had taken Braylon on a helluva roller coaster ride. Getting very little sleep, he fought hard as hell to keep his eyes open while working. He raked his fingers over the keyboard as tension coursed through his body, his watery eyes strained.

An expletive entered his mind. "This is useless," he said, reclining in his chair. He swiveled the chair to stare out the window.

A set of cumulus clouds floated over the shining sun. Across the street, CMC General Davidson led a unit run. The trainees trekking behind him were clad in their green track suits with gold and scarlet "Marines" lettering. As the unit started to disappear into the distance, Braylon's eyes honed in on the man jogging and carrying the American flag.

"Rough night, I heard," a female said from behind. He recognized the sassy voice immediately. *Alyssa.*

He turned to find the officer pinning him with a sexy stare. Alyssa strode into his office dressed in a long-sleeve midnight blue coat with medals consolidating over her left chest area, a blue skirt, and a pair of navy pumps. Her brunette hair was pulled tight to the back of her head in a low bun, revealing the creamy texture of her flawless white skin.

"I don't know if *rough* is the right word to use to describe last night. So you heard all about it, huh?" Was it possible that Alyssa was Simon? Every time he turned around here she was.

Without his permission, she closed the door. "Yes, I did. And that's why I came to see you."

"Oh."

She closed in on him, stopping when she reached the other side of his desk. "Rumor has it that you're dating Sandella Summers."

He clasped his fingers on his desk. How in the hell did she know this? he wondered, sizing her up, thinking Alyssa more than likely was Simon. "My personal life is just that Alyssa…personal."

"I'm not here to get into your personal life. I'm here to warn you."

"Warn me about what?"

"If you're thinking about reopening any closed cases, don't," she said bluntly. "The last person that did died." She waltzed around the corner of his desk, put her mouth to his ear, and whispered, "I wouldn't want to see a handsome thing like you end up dead and buried under the ground."

Braylon got to his feet in a quick fluid movement. Wickedness gleamed in her dark eyes. His heart twisted with disdain. "Is that a threat, Alyssa?" he said, clenching his jaws. *Or should I call you Simon?*

She leaned closer to him until her big boobs threatened to graze his chest. "No, it's not a threat, Wexler." With her pink lips slightly parted, her head descended forward as if she were about to kiss him. He quickly took a few steps backward to put space between them. Her lips spread across her face into a bright white smile. "You really are in love with Sandella, huh?"

Damn right I am! he wanted to scream, shocking the hell out of his own self. "Goodbye, Alyssa."

She pivoted on her heels and crossed the room, and when her hand grasped the knob, she turned back to look at him. "Why would you want a boring, plain Jane like Sandella, when you can have someone like me?" She blew him a kiss, then left.

A part of him had been tempted to defend Sandella. But considering Alyssa wasn't even important enough for him to care about the ugly words sputtering from her wicked mouth, he decided to let it go.

He shut his door, rounded the corner, and headed down the hallway. From where Braylon stood, Alyssa appeared to be a narcissist. Sure she was sexy, and attractive, and from what he'd heard…smart. But he already had what he wanted—Sandella. And as soon as he wrapped up this case, he was going to make her his—maybe even permanently.

The only thing that could stop him from taking things with Sandella to the next level was Drayton. If the kid turned out to be his, then he'd have no choice but to focus all his energy and attention on the child. Hell, he'd already missed three precious years of the boy's life.

Which reminded him, he needed to call his physician and make sure his blood work had been received by the DNA lab. Originally he'd planned on traveling to do the test, but time just hadn't been on his side to do so. Thank goodness Madison had cooperated and agreed that this way was best.

At first, Madison had wanted to select the doctor to conduct the paternity test, but since he didn't trust her, he'd insisted she let him make his own choice, a doctor who happened to be a great friend of the Wexler family. As much as he'd hate to lose Sandella over this, it would be nice to have a son.

Braylon opened the bathroom door and bumped into his boss.

"I was just coming to see you," Forest's deep voice echoed.

"You were? What about?" *Damn, what if Forest is Simon?*

"In my office now, Wexler." He stalked past him then held the door wide open for him to exit.

Can I at least take a piss first? Braylon followed Forest as he led him toward his office. Once inside the room overlooking the marsh, Forest closed the door behind him.

"I'm gone cut straight to the chase here, Wexler." He paused. "I know you've been reinvestigating the Summers case even after I warned you not too. My thought is to fire you, but I'd like to hear your reasoning first."

"Technically, sir, I wouldn't say that I've been investigating the Summers case."

Forest's bushy eyebrows hiked. "Tell me if I'm wrong here, Wexler." He wagged his finger. "But didn't you just outright go see Mrs. Theresa Jackson a few days ago?"

"Yes."

"And since then," his face contorted as he cleared his throat, "please excuse my French," he put his hands on his hips, "...but a shitload of shit has been happening since you've gone and done such a stupid thing. Let me make myself clear. Leave well enough alone." His voice was raspy. "Catch my drift?" he asked, lifting his right brow.

Braylon nodded. "I hear what you're saying...loud and clear, sir."

"Good. Consider this a warning. And just so you know I don't give warnings twice. You may leave now."

Knots pained Braylon's shoulders as he made his way back to the mailroom. If he didn't know any better, he'd think Forest had followed him to Theresa's house. Shoot, for all he knew, Forest might be keeping track of his every single move, and everything he researched on his computer. But just because his boss had warned him to leave well enough alone didn't mean squat to him. He'd been hardheaded all his life. And now that he'd promised Kane he'd seek justice, and wouldn't be able to see Sandella unless he did so, he definitely wasn't going to stop here.

He reached inside his mailbox and retrieved a certified letter addressed to him. Presuming this was another letter from Simon; he broke the seal, unfolded the letter, then started reading it. As usual, the letter was typed.

Dear Detective Wexler,

Because of my horrible experiences here on base, I often get terrified and have trouble sleeping most nights. In search of something to put me to sleep, I got up to drive to Walmart. On my way there, just as I turned the corner, I spotted a man pulling his car in the woods behind Mr. Crow's store.

Witnessing this, I quickly cut my lights and parked at the curb. When the man didn't come out of the woods, I decided to pull around and drive along the front of the street.

The next thing I knew, Theresa's house caught on fire. I started honking my horn to wake her. Thankfully, her neighbor came to her rescue.

Because I had a gut feeling the same man that'd entered the woods was the same person who'd set the fire, I made a quick u turn and drove in a hurry back to the neighborhood corner store. And sure enough, the same car I'd seen only minutes earlier came gunning from the woods, sped down the road, and came close to colliding with another car as it vanished.

I tried to get a tag number, but there wasn't one.
Simon.

Braylon blew out a harsh breath. With the letter still in his hand, he reclined his head on the top of his chair and peered up at the ceiling. So far, every letter he'd received from Simon had been checked for fingerprints and there hadn't been any. He'd even found out that the letters weren't coming from any of the local post offices, but from somewhere in Virginia.

He folded the letter and slid it back in the envelope. And because he didn't know if his phone or computer was being tampered with, he made his way outdoors, hopped in his Hummer, and drove to a place where he knew he'd have some privacy— home.

FORTY-FIVE MINUTES LATER, BACK AT the guest cottage, Braylon sat on the stool at the kitchen table surfing the computer, more specifically the registry of deeds. Talk about getting lucky, Braylon thought, stumbling across a vital piece of information linking Forest to several rental properties close to Mr. Crow's store.

Braylon keyed in the addresses for the first two properties Forest owned. Nothing unique or off stood out to him. "What am I missing? What am I not seeing?" He talked to himself, typing in the last address.

When the last address popped up on the map, burning anger shot through his fucking veins. Just to make sure his eyes weren't playing tricks on him, he reread the address It read, *3583 Claxton Ave.* "Oh...my...God." He shut his stinging eyes, then reopened them.

Forest owned a home directly behind Sandella's house. They were back-door neighbors. Other than a few short trees nothing separated the two houses. Although he'd promised Kane he'd stay away from her until he found Sugar's killer, he wasn't going to stand by and do nothing to protect her. *To hell with that.* Already there'd been one too many threats on her life.

He snatched his keys from the counter and hastened across the living room. When he opened the front door, he took a step back. Sandella, her father, and three more men stood on his porch. Sandella looked exactly like the tallest guy.

"Hi." Sandella's sweet lips curved into a smile. "My brothers insisted that they meet you today."

Braylon hoped his eyes were smiling, because his heart sure wasn't. *Forest owns the house behind hers.* "I was just on my way to see you."

"I'm glad to save you the trouble."

"Coming to see you is never any trouble." If her family members hadn't been there he would've pulled her into his arms and cradled her up against his chest, then planted his tongue deep inside her throat.

"I know you!" the youngest boy of the crew shouted.

It didn't take but a second for Braylon to recognize the kid, but he couldn't quite place his name. "Yes. I worked with you at the youth center last week."

Kane's eyes looked softer today than they did last night. He turned to his youngest son. "This is the guy you've been ranting and raving about?"

Sandella turned to look at her baby brother. "Is he the one that taught you how to change the tire?"

"Yes. He taught me how to tie a bowtie for a tuxedo, too."

Her eyes gleamed at the fact he'd been helping her brother. "Small. Small world."

As Sandella made the introductions, Braylon gave each of the men, including Kane and Drew, a firm shake.

"Come in."

Kane rolled his wheelchair inside the comfort of the cottage with his sons following close behind him. "We wanted to meet with you," Chandler, the oldest brother, said, "to give you—"

Kane cleared his throat. "Let me tell him."

Braylon slid his hands in his pockets. *I don't know if I want to hear this.*

Kane said, "I wanted to give you my blessing, in person, to date my daughter." His sudden change of heart stunned Braylon. "I can't explain it, but there's something about you that's all right with me."

"But if you hurt her," Chandler started up again, "you're going to have to answer to all four of us."

"Ditto," Aric put in his two cents.

"Ya'll need to ease up on the brotha," Drew commented. "Sandy's a grown woman and she can take care of herself."

Sandella chuckled. "That's right. Tell them Drew."

Braylon draped an arm around Sandella's shoulder. "I have no intentions of ever hurting Sandella." But the situation concerning Drayton might do exactly that—hurt her. *Damn.*

A sheen of doubt settled deep inside Kane's eyeballs. "By the way...thanks for helping my Sandy start up SugarKanes."

Braylon finally smiled. "The pleasure is all mine, Mr. Summers."

"Kane...call me Kane."

"Will do, sir." Braylon didn't know how to break the sullen news to the men and Sandella, but he had no choice. "While I appreciate you all giving me your blessings, I have no intentions of taking you up on your offer at the present time."

Sandella's smiling lips turned down. "What are you saying?"

"Sandella...I'm the type of man that keeps my promises. I promised your father I wouldn't be with you until I arrested your mother's killer, and I meant it."

Sandella's eyes blinked profusely. "You can't be serious."

"I was on my way to see you because...for reasons I can't get into...I feel your life is in great jeopardy." He diverted his eyes to Kane. "I don't want her staying with you until the case is resolved. I don't even want her visiting unless you're home."

Kane shook his head. He drew a cigarette from his pocket,

slapped it between his tongue and jaw. He then withdrew it, not bothering to light it. "If you know something, you better go and tell it, damn it!"

"He can't, Dad," Chandler said.

"Like hell he can't!" Kane retorted.

Aric put a hand on his father's shoulder. "As a criminal investigator, there are certain things he's not at liberty to say."

"Well, if he's sleeping with my damn daughter that shit should be out the damn window. Ain't no such thing as privacy when you sharing your bed with somebody."

"Daaadd!" Sandella shouted.

"Cool it, Dad!" Chandler spoke out. "The man is just doing his job."

The room fell silent until Kane broke the ice. "Well, where should she stay then?"

"She can keep staying here," Braylon suggested. "Even after my grandmother and grandfather return, I want her here."

Kane muttered, "Didn't you just say you weren't going to see her until the case was resolved?"

I meant making love to her. "I view dating and seeing as two different things."

Kane's eyes rolled. "If you say so."

"When I'm not here during the day there'll be a cop posted outside the estate for her protection."

"And if I need to leave?" Sandella questioned.

"Try not to leave unless it's absolute necessary."

Sandella's cell buzzed. She reached inside her purse, tapped the button, then placed it on her ear. "Hello." She gasped. Her face twisted. "He wants to talk to you," she said, handing Braylon the phone.

"Hello?"

"She's one dead bitch," the man on the other end threatened in a deep chilling voice, then hung up.

Braylon's heart wrung like a twisting washcloth in his chest.

Chapter Twelve

INSIDE THE MAIN HOUSE, BRAYLON positioned his eye over the peephole and spied across the street beneath the large oak. Officer Jeff Thompson was sitting inside his unmarked vehicle keeping a close watch on the estate for possible endangerment. The undercover cop's back straightened as a Mercedes with gleaming headlights sailed past him along the dark road.

"I wish you didn't have to leave right now," Sandella said sullenly from behind. As he turned to face her she fully entered the living room. Wearing a thin brown sweater and dark jeans, she slid her hands into her pockets, coming to a stop in front of him.

Braylon put a finger under her chin, tilting her head. "I know you're scared, but you'll be fine. Jeff is right outside and he's not going to let anything happen to you or Royce." He pecked her lips.

Nodding, she began rubbing her arms. "How long will you be gone?"

"I don't know."

"Be careful."

"Always. Lock the doors." Braylon gently kissed her cheek,

then left.

CLOSE TO THIRTY MINUTES LATER, Braylon drove his Hummer into the vacant spot in front of his office building and parked. With Forest possibly monitoring his every move, he'd decided to return to work well after the majority of the employees were gone and were hopefully at home in their beds asleep.

He mounted the steps. *What is Forest hiding? The caller sounded nothing like him.* He typed his security number into the keypad and the locked door clicked open.

Close to midnight, he entered the quiet dark building to find it empty, even eerie. He rounded his secretary's desk, strode past his office, then stalked down the long murky hallway toward the storage area where all the original case files were kept.

Coming to a stop in front of the steel door, he punched in his security code. *Beeeep.* The alarm purred, disarming the airtight security. He proceeded inside, shutting the door behind him.

Turning on the bright lights might signal others that he was inside so he left them off. Although he had a right to be in this room, Forest had a way of making him feel like he didn't. Row after row of tall silver shelves filled the cold room.

I need to see the original file. Walking between the tight crevices of two shelves on either side, he whipped out his flashlight. Aiming high, he shined the bright beam of light on several white boxes, before finding the one he came to review—Case Number **VI78591658**.

He reached up high, retracted the box from the shelf, then placed it on the floor. Kneeling, he lifted the lid, and pulled out the original case file belonging to a woman by the name of Victoria Varn. He started perusing the sheets of paper.

Earlier today, right after he'd received the threatening phone call that'd terrified Sandella, he dug harder into the investigation, and had stumbled across several pieces of pertinent information.

Over a year ago, a woman by the name of Victoria had filed a complaint stating she'd been kidnapped on base, taken to Forest's home that sat behind Sandella's house, and had been brutally raped.

However, at the time of the unfortunate incident, the rental property had been vacant. Kane probably had no clue about any of this because the occurrence never went public. After everything his family had gone through, Sandella, Kane, and her brothers deserved to know their home sat directly behind that of a monster.

His shoulders felt heavy as he scrutinized the old worn papers which smelled like a combination of grass and acid. Forest investigating the case was nothing new, he thought, reading his signature at the bottom of the report. *It's a damn shame he investigated a crime that took place at his own home. No one probably knows he owns several properties.*

Braylon paused when he stumbled across a sheet of paper containing Victoria's middle name—*Victoria Simone Varn. Simone. Simone. Drop the e—Simon?*

So this Victoria Varn woman was his Simon?

He flipped to the next sheet of paper in the disorderly stack. As soon as he saw the picture of the female victim stamped in the upper right corner, he swore. A wave of nausea rose to the surface of his gut. *Damn.* The woman in the photo was his secretary. First thing tomorrow morning he and his secretary, Victoria, were going to have a serious, difficult conversation.

Her last name is Wilkins now. So Varn has to be her maiden name.

The report concluded with Victoria stating the rapist had worn a mask, preventing her from seeing her attacker's face. But she did verify a spider tattoo on the lower right side of his abdomen.

A spider tattoo? I wonder if Forest has a spider tattoo? Sick over the incriminating evidence, Braylon growled as he tucked the box back on the shelf.

As he made his way back outdoors, a sudden occurrence surged inside his brain. Forest's youngest son, Todd, had been the last person to live inside the home. *I wonder if Todd has a spider tattoo?*

EARLY SATURDAY MORNING BRAYLON STOOD on Victoria's front porch knocking on the screen door. A small two-stall barn sat positioned to the right of the home while a large muddy creek known to produce oysters nestled in the depths of the earth behind it. He'd heard all about the summer seafood fests out here on Lady's Island.

The door creaked open. He turned to find Victoria standing there in a long, fluffy pink robe. "Braylon. What brings you here?" she asked, standing on the other side of the screen door. "I think you know why I'm here, Victoria. May I please come in?"

Victoria pushed the door back and stepped to the side. The sweet smell of cinnamon buns streamed up his nose. The inside of her home was just as cozy and as interesting as the outside. A bright beautiful portrait of a woman wearing a yellow sundress clung to her wall above a white sofa.

"I'm sorry to interrupt your Saturday, but what I have to ask you is too important to wait until Monday."

Her eyes traveled south. She slid her hands inside the pockets of her robe, then looked back up at him. "I just finished baking some cinnamon rolls, would you like one?" she asked, as if trying to stall the inevitable.

"No thanks. Victoria…I know you're Simon. I also know that you were raped. As hard as this may be, I want you to tell me wh—"

"It happened last year on Halloween," she interjected. She sat down on the couch and clasped her fingers together. "Alyssa Carrington invited me to a Halloween party. She said she'd pick me up at the corner where Alpine and Alcorn met. So the evening of the party I went there and waited for her."

Alyssa? I knew she was no good.

Victoria continued. "When she'd said to meet her there, I found it rather odd because it's so dark and isolated at the back of the base. But because she was my friend at the time, I trusted it to be okay. I should've followed my instincts." She swallowed.

VICTORIA'S HEART THREATENED TO SPLINTER like wood in her tight chest. Sitting across from the detective, she nervously wrung her hands. She knew the smart man would eventually come knocking on her door to question her. Thing is, she had no clue it'd happen this soon. But yet, this is what she'd been praying for—for him to come.

She sighed. *I can do this.* A tear formed in the bottom rim of her eye as she began telling her side of the story about the night she'd been raped. She parted her mouth to speak and the words took their time coming out. "I decided to go as Snow White to the Halloween party. I was standing on the corner—"

Standing on the dark corner beneath a dim light post and dressed like Snow White, the cool night air briskly feathered Victoria's cheeks. As she waited for her girlfriend Alyssa Carrington to come get her, a feeling of uneasiness swept over her. Contemplating if she should leave, she nibbled her bottom lip. Where was Alyssa?

As the scent of the peppery marsh close by wafted up her nose, the lamp post above her head suddenly blinked off. Anxiety coursed through her making her wish she'd never committed to attending the Halloween party.

Just as she put one foot forth to leave, a car turned the corner then slowly drove toward her. The gleaming headlights on the car shinned brightly into her eyes, completely blinding her. She squinted.

Happy because Alyssa had finally arrived, a big smile curved Victoria's lips. When the car came to a stop in front of her, Alyssa rolled down the passenger side window, and smiled. "Get in."

"About time you get here. What took you so long?" Victoria asked, wondering who was sitting in the driver's seat. Alyssa hadn't mentioned someone else would be joining them this evening.

Victoria hooked her hand under the car handle opening the door. As soon as she slid on the seat in the rear someone bagged her head, suffocating her. She screamed only to swallow her own terrifying sounds.

As her attacker dragged her from the back seat of the car, her legs and arms flailed wildly. He tossed her in the trunk, drove off, and long minutes later she ended up at the house on Claxton.

As her attacker forced her up the steps of the home, he pressed the tip of a sharp blade to her spine. Tears were streaming rapidly down her face. He opened the door, shoved her down the hallway toward the bedroom.

Once inside the cold musky room, he snatched the bag off her head. "Turn around." He snorted.

Victoria slowly turned around to face him to find he was wearing a black mask to shield his face. The room was so dark, but if she had to guess, she'd say his eyes were a light green just like Forest's.

The green-eyed monster lifted the shining blade to her cheek and traced it down to her abdomen. She shivered with fear. The whole time she kept thinking why did Alyssa do this to her. Why? Why? Why? From what she could tell Alyssa was nowhere to be found. Maybe she'd gotten out of the car before it'd taken off.

With the tip of the sharp blade now pressed to the base of her throat, he shoved her back on the bed, zipped down his pants, and that's when she spotted the red spider tattoo with the same green eyes as him on his abdomen.

After he violently took her, he re-covered her head, and hauled her outside. Once her feet left the steps, she sneakily dropped her red costume bracelet on the ground. Then she counted every step she took, and every turn she made.

The sticks snapped beneath her red shiny shoes as they went further out into the woods. "Stop here," the rapist had ordered. When he'd given her permission to stop walking, she just knew her life was over. That she was going to die out in the dark, cold forest. "Count to one hundred, then you can leave," was all he said.

As fear sliced her heart in half she proceeded to count. Once she reached one hundred and one, she removed the bag from her head, and had no clue where she was.

Victoria swiped a tear from her eye. "So I just ran as fast as I could and ended up behind Mr. Crow's old store. Because it was Halloween he was still there passing out candy to the children in the neighborhood. He took me inside and called the police."

Braylon jotted down the details inside his leather pad, then lifted his gaze to meet her tortured eyes. "Did you ever confront Alyssa about why she left you?"

"Yes."

"And what did she say?"

"She said it was a joke. That he was supposed to take me in the woods, but the rape was never part of the plan. When I asked her who'd done this to me, she refused to give me a name. She said he'd threatened to kill her if she did."

"Alyssa needs to own up to her part in this."

"I think she was about to tell me right before Marc Jackson was murdered."

Braylon's face scrunched as he tucked his note pad into his pocket, then he stood. "Thanks for your time. Make sure you lock your doors, and be extremely careful, Victoria. Or shall I say,

Simon?" A light chuckle rolled off his lips.

Victoria smiled. "Victoria is fine."

"Call me if you think of anything else." He crossed the living room to the front door.

"There is one more thing." Braylon paused in his tracks, then he turned to face her. She continued. "Over the last three years...there's been a rape in Beaufort every Halloween night."

"Halloween?"

"Tonight," Victoria confirmed.

Braylon sprang into action.

Chapter Thirteen

"BUT EVERYONE IS GOING TO be there!" Drew's voice pinched Sandella's eardrums as she stood in her father's living room observing the affronting look slanting her baby brother's face. "Please, Dad? I never get to do anything." Drew pouted, looking down at his father. "Living here is worse than being in prison."

"Like hell this is jail." Kane snarled. "When I was growing up—"

"But times have changed," Drew cut his father off. "Man, everyone at school is going to be there. It's the biggest party of the year."

Kane scowled. "You're not going!"

Drew sucked his teeth. "Sandy! Please!"

Kane shook his head vigorously. "She's not your mother, son."

Sandella quickly covered her ears. "All right. All right," she said, folding her arms across her breasts. "Dad, he has a good point."

Her father's eyes rolled. "Like hell he does."

"Colonel Barton has had the Halloween party for the last three years. His kids attend Beaufort High with Drew. It'll be good for him to be around his friends."

"I don't like this, Sandy." Kane grumbled.

"He's a junior, Dad. One more year, and he'll be an adult." She patted Drew's back. "He's old enough to know right from wrong, and he hasn't done anything for us not to trust him. I think you should give him an opportunity to prove himself."

Kane lit his cigarette, then drew in a deep breath. Hot smoke spiraled from his dark, full lips. "You better not disappoint me, son."

Drew's eyes beamed with exhilaration. "Thanks, Dad!"

"If you pick him up, I'll be more than happy to drop him off." Kane peered up at Drew. "Be ready to leave by eleven thirty."

Drew threw up his hands. "Eleven thirty? But it's not over until twelve."

"Okay, well make that ten, then." Kane curled his lips around his cigarette.

Drew relented. "Never mind. Eleven thirty is fine with me," he said, then took off down the hallway.

Sandella's heart warmed from her father's willingness to compromise. "Let me go finish cooking." She waltzed inside the kitchen to the stove, lifted the lid from the pot, and inhaled the spicy aroma of seafood jambalaya.

The timer on the stove chirped. *Mmm.* She slid the large baking dish containing fresh tilapia stuffed with lump crabmeat out of the oven and placed it on the stove.

"Dad! Drew! Dinner's ready!" After fixing her father's plate, she placed it on the table, then crossed the kitchen to the window. As she stood over the sink observing the dark starless sky, her mind drifted to Braylon.

Earlier this morning, she'd tried to seduce him, and he'd turned down her advances. He'd stated he intended to keep his promise to her father. He wouldn't touch her until he found her mother's killer. The more she thought about his promise, the more she disliked it. What if he never captured the killer? Then what? She couldn't fathom living a life without Braylon. The thought pained her heart.

Just as she stuck her hands into the warm bubbly dish water, her old neighbor, Buddy Greene, appeared on the porch at the house behind hers. He turned a beer bottle up to his lips, swallowed, then tossed it in the bin. Was he back? she wondered, scrubbing the pot. God, she sure hoped not.

Bud had resided behind her father's house a few years back and he'd been the worst neighbor ever. He'd nearly driven her mother crazy with all the loud country music and wild drunken fests he'd held at his home on many late nights. At one point her mother had gotten so upset until she'd called the police on him. Afterward, he'd moved out, and she hadn't seen or heard from him until now.

Bud descended the steps and started crossing the lawn toward her home.

Oh God, here he comes. Sandella pulled her hands from the warm water and as she dried them on the dish towel, a loud knock resounded on the back door.

She pulled open the back door. Bud's striking green eyes sparkled when they met hers. He stood beneath the porch light wearing a wrinkled plain white t-shirt and a pair of blue jeans. A myriad of tattoos covered his body. The black dragon tattoo on his neck had the same color eyes as he did. So did the tattoo of the woman inked down the length of his right arm.

"Sorry to interrupt you," he said, his fierce green eyes raking up and down her body, "but I was just about to make dinner when I noticed I needed an onion. Do you by any chance have one?"

An onion? Really? "I'm sorry, but I don't," she lied, feeling extremely uncomfortable around him. "Have you moved back in?" *Please say no.*

"Yep. Sure have."

Darn. "What brings you back?"

"My father decided to rent out the property I was living in to a family of four. He's all about making that money, and I don't blame him in the least bit." He shifted sideways to look back at his home. "Considering it's just me, this house fits my needs better anyway. The other place was way too big for just one person."

"Who's there?" Kane said, wheeling himself into the kitchen.

"It's Bud from—"

Kane interjected, "What do you want?"

"Just came to borrow an onion, that's all."

"Well, we don't have any."

His green eyes scraped down to Sandella's breasts then lifted back to her face. Thank God her father was sitting behind her and hadn't seen the look of lust in Bud's eyes. "That's what this pretty gal of yours was just telling me."

"Watch your mouth, boy."

"Just giving a compliment...that's all. Sorry to interrupt your dinner. Y'all be good now, you hear?"

"Have a nice evening." Sandella closed the door. She then turned around to find her father clenching his jaws.

Kane's eyes grew darker as he said, "There's something about that man I just don't like. Don't open up my door for him anymore. And keep the gun I bought you with you at all times. You got that?"

Although she'd left the weapon at Willa's, she'd plan to keep it with her from this night forward. "Yes. Bud gives me the creeps too. He—"

"I'm ready!" Drew jumped into the kitchen with his arms spread wide wearing a homemade Halloween costume. He'd caked his face with white powder, painted his lips red, and had taken her eyeliner from her purse to draw big black circles around both his eyes.

Sandella looked at her father and they both burst into wild

laughter. "And who are you supposed to be?" she asked, grinning.

Drew shrugged as if they should recognize his character. "I'm the Joker from Batman."

"If you want, I can run you to the store and pick up a costume."

"Thanks, but I'm good just like this. Let's go."

"Not until after you eat dinner," Sandella came back, still feeling uncomfortable about Bud.

"But—"

"No buts—" Her cell buzzed against her hip. She reached inside her pocket to pull out her phone. The name on the screen brought a smile to her face. It was Braylon. "Hello."

"Where are you?"

"I'm at my father's."

"Is he there?"

"Yes. I just came over here to cook dinner. As a matter of fact, I'm on my way back to the estate in a few minutes. Adam is watching Royce for me, and he has a date tonight, so I'm kind of in a hurry."

"The sooner you get back, the better. Officer Thompson is on his way over here now. May I speak with your father?"

Sandella placed her hand over the cell's speaker. "It's Braylon. He wants to speak with you."

A dazed expression appeared on Kane's face as he reached for the phone. "Hello." It'd taken all of thirty seconds for them to speak with one another. When Kane was done conversing with her lover, he handed her the phone.

"What did he want?" she asked, slipping the cell back into her pocket.

"He didn't say. All he said was he needed to speak with me in private. He's on his way over."

TWENTY MINUTES LATER, SANDELLA PULLED up on the curb of Colonel Barton's home with Drew in costume in the passenger's seat. "Have fun...and be good," Sandella advised, smiling.

"Always." Drew flung open the door, hopped out of the car, and walked coolly toward the front door. When he was halfway there, the front door suddenly flung open. Two teenage girls happily rushed up to him and bestowed him with a group hug. Her little brother was definitely growing up, she thought, smiling, then pulling away. *What does Braylon want to talk to my father about? It must be about the case.*

After making a left turn at the stop sign, she made a quick right then proceeded to drive down the long dark road. A love song streamed from the car speakers, serenading her. Memories of the way Braylon had once sucked her throbbing clitoris into his hot mouth came cruising into her mind. Her nipples tightened beneath the fabric of her satin bra. Sizzling heat gathered in her core. *Oh my,* it was throbbing.

She missed the feel of his long thick column buried inside her, pumping her, his sperm filling her to the hilt. The last time they'd made hot, steamy love, he'd cupped her buttocks and brought her sex up to his mouth. Then he'd trailed his tongue along the flesh of her labia before slipping it into her soaked entrance. He'd nibbled on her throbbing pearl, and had—

Red and blue lights flashing in her rearview mirror interrupted her sweet, sensual memories. The siren on the police vehicle whooped, then the cop car closed in on her. Darn, had she been speeding? She nervously pulled over to the side of the road.

As the officer strode toward her car, her pulse beat hard in her throat. She'd never received a ticket before. Once he reached her window, she hit the button, and the tinted glass rolled down.

When the officer ducked his head and leveled his striking green gaze with hers, her heart dipped. He wrapped his strong hands around her neck, squeezed, then slapped a strong-smelling rag over her mouth and nose.

Trying to ward him off, she dug her nails into the skin of his arm and tried to pry his forceful hand from her gagging mouth. As she fought to take her next breath, her vision blurred. Why had she been stupid and refused to carry the gun her father had given her? Everything in sight suddenly faded to black.

Chapter Fourteen

KANE EYED BRAYLON SPECULATIVELY AS he towered over him. "I'm not moving out of my own damn house unless you give me a good enough reason," his voice boomed, confusion bouncing around in his hooded eyes.

Braylon had figured Kane would say as much. "I can't give you specifics, but I have reason to believe the person who killed your wife may live close by." *Very close.*

Hitching his brows, Kane leaned forward. "How damn close?" He squinted.

"Let's just say it'd be in your family's best interests to move for a while."

Kane shook his head. "I'm not going to let no devil of a man run me out of my own god damn house. If he even thinks about showing up here, before he even steps over the threshold, he'll find out I'm no pussy." Kane reached down in his pants and pulled out a pistol. "Braylon, meet Blaze." He kissed the tip of the barrel. "Blaze here will fire a hot bullet in someone's ass before they can blink an eye."

Braylon should've known better than to try and convince a stubborn man like Kane to leave his own home. Truth was, he didn't think he'd do it anyhow. But because he didn't want Sandella over there at all, including in the daytime, he'd decided to give it a shot. "Just promise me you won't use the gun unless your life is in jeopardy and it's absolutely necessary."

"I thought I was gone have to use it earlier today," he said, lowering the pistol to the table.

Braylon's overloaded mind jumped on the information he'd found out earlier today after he'd left Victoria Varn's home. Come to find out, one of Forest's rental properties recently became available. For the last three Halloweens, a rape had occurred at one of his available properties.

The disturbing way local authorities had overlooked this mishap frustrated the fuck out of Braylon. Someone was covering up for Forest? Who? And why?

Kane cleared his throat, jarring Braylon from his deep thoughts. He then continued. "He just looked like he was up to no good. I could see it in those evil green eyes of his. I've always been a good people reader, and something ain't right about him. Talking about he needed a damn onion."

"Who?"

"Bud. He's moved back into the house right behind me."

Buddy Greene is back. Fuck! "And he came to visit you today?" Braylon's mind whirled.

"Not visit. He showed up on my back porch claiming he needed to borrow an onion. Mr. Crow's store is right there on the corner, and it wouldn't take him any time to get there. I think he came here to get fresh with Sandy."

Braylon's gut churned violently. The fact that Bud had showed up for no good reason had his temples bulging. "I—" His cell phone buzzed. "Excuse me," he said, pulling it from his clip. "Everything okay?" he queried Officer Jeff Thompson.

"I don't know. I'm here at the Wexlers' estate and Sandella hasn't showed up yet. Adam is here with Royce, and he said he hasn't heard from her."

"Let me follow up with that," he said in a calm tone, not wanting to alarm Kane. "As soon as I find out something, I'll call you."

"Likewise."

Braylon ended the call and as he hurried toward the front door, Kane wheeled behind him. "If you change your mind about moving out to the estate, please let me know. In the meantime lock up."

"Thanks for offering and for your concern, but Blaze and I are staying right here."

Now inside the car, Braylon threw the car in reverse, sped out of Kane's driveway, and headed for the vacant rental property Forest owned. His stomach wrenched with anxiety as he dialed Sandella's cell. The phone chirped in his ear eight times before he finally hung up.

With fists clenching the steering wheel, he zoomed across the bridge. If his theory was correct, Sandella was in grave, grave danger. Horrific thoughts coursed through his brain threatening to make his heart collapse.

DRUGGED OUT OF HER MIND, Sandella felt her body lifting from the trunk of the car. Then it seemed as if she was floating in the air. The sound of branches snapping beneath a pair of hard shoes assailed her ears. Her captor was carrying her through the woods.

With her eyes closed, she swayed her head side to side struggling to fully awaken. She then forced her eyes open. Her blurred vision fought hard to stabilize as she focused in on the half-moon glowing in the sky. Then her eyes honed in on the masked man toting her.

A horrid memory attacked her mind. She'd been taken against her will. Bile into her throat. As the man mounted the steps to the house surrounded by woods, the floorboards creaked.

"You're awake." His dark, throaty voice terrified her and she shivered. When he pulled open the heavy wooden door, it gave off a resounding squeak. He stepped over the threshold and kicked the door closed behind them.

Inside the house reeked of mothballs. He strode past a brick fireplace, rounded a corner to the left, then ended up inside a dark bedroom. He switched on the light.

"Whyyyy me?" Sandella slurred.

He pinned her with a wicked green stare, then dropped her on the mattress. As he peered down at her, he tilted his head. "Why not you? Why not your mother?" He plopped down on top of her.

Sandella screamed. As her body writhed beneath his strong masculine build, she clawed at his face and snatched off his mask.

A lopsided grin was plastered on Buddy Greene's face. He reached between them and fumbled with his belt. The sound of his zipper lowering scraped her ears. *Oh God no. He's going to rape me.* "Heeellllp," she wailed.

"Are you as good as your mother?" Using rugged force, he pinned her arms above her head, then pried her thighs apart with his knee.

"Please don't do this," she wailed.

"I promise you'll like it." The stench of alcohol poured from his hot breath down on her face.

Fearing for her life, tears rolled down her eyes. Panic raced throughout her. Her legs went numb. Her body stilled. Fisting her hands, she braced herself for his assaults.

Pooowww! The sound of gunfire popped Sandella's eardrums. She glanced up and there was a big, black hole in the ceiling. With his jeans puddled around his hips, Bud jumped off of her.

Braylon stood at the end of the bed aiming his weapon at Bud's chest. "Did he hurt you?" His angry voice echoed, bouncing off the walls.

"No. Not yet," she cried, scrambling to her feet. She hurried to Braylon's side.

"Turn around and put your hands behind your back." Braylon reached into his holster and whipped out his handcuffs.

As Sandella stood behind Braylon shaking like a leaf, she noticed a spider tattoo on Bud's abdomen. He and the ugly creature had the same god-awful green eyes. "If it's okay with you, I'm going to button my pants first."

"It's not okay with me. Turn...your ass...around. Now," Braylon warned through clenched teeth.

With his hands behind his back, Bud slowly pivoted toward the wall. Braylon rushed up behind him and slapped the silver cuffs on his wrists. "I almost got away with it."

"But you didn't, son," a firm voice stated from behind.

BRAYLON WHIRLED TO FIND FOREST standing in the doorway pointing a gun at Braylon's chest. Keeping his weapon aimed at Forest's forehead, Braylon ordered, "Put the gun down, Forest."

Releasing a throaty grunt, Forest's face twisted. He then swiped the gun toward his son. "I warned you to stay out of trouble, Bud. Ever since you got fired from the police department, you've been nothing but a headache." His vivid green eyes darkened to a color resembling mushed peas.

Braylon stood in front of Sandella using his body as a protective shield. So Bud was an ex-cop? And Forest had been protecting him? "Put your gun down, Forest."

Forest continued, "The last time you went and done this, I told you that if you did it again, I wasn't going to have your back." Sweat gathered like a row of tiny raindrops on his forehead. "And I meant every god damn word...son."

Poooowww! Forest fired a bullet straight into Bud's skull and his brains splattered against the wall.

Braylon's finger squeezed the trigger firing off a round of hot lead into Forest's chest. Forest's gun tumbled from his loosened grip, and he plummeted to the floor. "Sorry for your troubles," he choked out, blood slipping from the crack of his lips, then shut his eyes for good.

Chapter Fifteen

BRAYLON'S FEET MOVED ACROSS THE carpet with urgency as he hastened toward the kitchen inside the cottage. His eyes expanded when he noticed the time on the clock. It was four fifteen in the afternoon. *Shit! I overslept.* Shaking his head, he swiped a heavy hand down his frowning face.

Last night's horrible events involving Forest and his son had worn him out, and had caused him to sleep as if he were hibernating. And now he was late picking up Sandella from the hospital. Hours late!

Just as he snatched his keys from the counter, the doorbell rang. When he plied the door open, joy gripped his heart and relief flooded through his veins. Sandella along with her father and brothers stood before him, smiling like they'd won the lottery.

"You did it, goddamnit!" Kane hooted, then rolled his wheelchair over the threshold. Sandella and her brothers followed. With his hands on his thighs, Kane tilted his head back and chuckled heartily. "You said you were going to find my Sugar's killer, and you got his psycho ass!" He slapped his thigh. "Now I can finally rest in peace. And so can my Sugar."

The light in Kane's eyes quickly faded to darkness. Then his bottom lip quivered. He continued. "Thank you for what you've done. My boys and I, and Sandy, are forever indebted to you, and I..." his voice trailed off as he choked on a sob.

Sandella patted her father's shoulder. "It's okay, Dad. Get it out." She transferred her eyes to Braylon. "We are so thankful for what you did for us." She batted her eyelashes and a single tear rolled down her face.

God, I love this woman. "Please don't mention it. I was just doing my job."

Chandler sniffed. "No. You went way above the call of duty. We can never repay you for what you did for us."

"Thank you," Aric said with tears in his eyes.

Before Braylon could part his lips to reply, Drew threw his arms around him and burst into tears. "He's finally gone pay for killing my momma!"

Braylon patted Drew's back. "Yes...he's going to jail for the rest of his life." There wasn't a set of dry eyes in the room, including Braylon's.

After everyone regained their composure, Sandella and her family sat chatting about the awful events until Kane finally said he was ready to go home. He thanked Braylon so many times he couldn't count the number even if he wanted. Right before the Summers men left, Kane reminded Braylon that he had his blessing to date Sandella. The fact that Kane had given him his blessing twice sent him to grinning.

Standing in the doorway gripping the frame, he watched in delight as Kane's truck backed out of the driveway. Happy to have brought Sandella and the men in her family closure, he shut the door. He plopped down on the couch next to her. "How are you feeling?"

She released a long yawn into the cupped hand covering her mouth. "Tired. Overwhelmed. I'm still a little shaken." She ran her hands up and down her arms like she was warding off the cold.

Braylon tilted her chin upward. "I'll never let a soul hurt you again. And that's a promise." He kissed her tender lips.

"They're almost finished with clearing the land on the ocean for the bakery," she said, changing the subject.

"That's wonderful."

"I still can't get over how fast SugarKanes has grown in such a short amount of time."

"With you in charge, anything is possible, baby." Braylon wrapped his arms around Sandella pulling her snuggly against his chest. "I love you so much." He kissed the top of her hair.

"I love you so much." She shut her eyes and, just as she began drifting off to sleep, the front door cracked open.

"Sandella! Are you okay?" Willa shouted, bursting inside the cottage with no warning.

"Why didn't you knock first, Willa?" Drake asked, appearing in the doorway.

Willa sucked in a breath. "Aw, be quiet Drake. You always got to be so formal about everything."

Sandella sprung from Braylon's embrace, darted straight into Willa's open arms, and nestled her head up against her bosom like the child Willa treated her as. "I'm so glad you're finally home."

With her chin pressed to the top of Sandella's head, Willa closed her eyes. "Me too, darling. I'm so happy to be home."

TWO WEEKS LATER, WEARING A life vest, Braylon climbed down from the river dock behind his grandparents' estate, then lowered himself onto the seat of his brand new Yamaha jet ski. Gripping the handle bars, he peered up at Sandella. "Hop on," he invited, instantly thinking about how he'd like for her to hop on and ride his rod, too. A big smile developed on his face.

Smiling down at him, she tightened the straps on her orange life vest. "Are you thinking what I think you're thinking?" she asked, wrapping her arms around his waist.

Braylon started the engine on his new toy. "If you're thinking that I can't wait to fuck you, then yeah, that's what I'm thinking."

"Is that all you ever think about?" Inhaling his spicy cologne, she looked out at the water, and relished the way her breasts felt mashed into his spine. God, he was so manly.

"For the most part, yeah." He rotated the gear and the jet ski skidded across the river.

Cold water kicked up from the depths of the ocean splattering her face. Enjoying the cool breeze nipping at her, she held on tight. *Wheeee! This is so much fun.* Braylon had mentioned he had something to show her, but she had no idea what it was. The craft zipped toward Harbor Island.

Minutes later they came to a complete stop in front of the big white house they'd visited months prior. Braylon climbed off the Jet Ski, reached for her hand, and pulled her toward him. Making their way toward the breathtaking home, they walked hand in hand.

After they dismounted the dock, Braylon released a sigh, then smiled. "This is what I wanted to show you." She felt his grip tighten on her hand.

"Why did you want to show me Clyde's house?"

He reached in his pocket, then dangled a key before her eyes. "This isn't Clyde's house anymore. It's mine."

Sandella gasped. She smiled. "You bought it?"

He nodded. "Yes. I bought it for us."

Thinking she'd heard wrong, she touched a hand to her heart. "For us?" As Braylon reached inside his other pocket, light tremors enveloped her body. *Us. Oh God. Is he about to...*

"Yes us," he reiterated, holding a tiny Tiffany box in his large palm. Shocked, she covered her mouth to swallow the cry of joy threatening to depart from her lungs. He got down on one knee in front of her. Then he peeled open the box. Inside lay a beautiful, sparkling ring. The breathtaking diamond was round, and it was set in platinum, and it looked like it cost a fortune.

Her fingers trembled over her quivering lips as she peered down at him. "Oh, Braylon. What are you doing?"

"I love you so much, baby." He swallowed. "It'd do my heart some good," he patted over his heart area, "if you'll say yes and marry me. I want you to be my wife."

I can't believe this. Sniffing, she nodded. When she placed a gentle hand on the side of his face, he turned his head to kiss the inside of her palm. She felt the weight of tears on her blinking eyelashes. "Yes. I'd love to be your wife."

A big grin spread across his face. He jumped to his feet, slid the ring on her finger, then slipped his tongue inside her mouth.

"Let's go see our new house!" He grabbed her hand and they took off running.

Long minutes later, after they toured the empty house, they wound up in the bare family room beside the fireplace. Sandella twined her arms around his neck and stared into his warm gaze. "I've been waiting to do something all day."

His right brow arched. "What?"

"This." She reached inside his pants and fisted his cock.

He emitted a deep moan. He put his nose to hers. "I love it when you touch me." As she stroked his member it hardened within her velvety grip. "Oh, that feels good." Her strong jerking hand seemed to inflame him.

Standing in front of her, he gripped her shoulders, then made her walk backward until her spine touched the wall. His fingers swiftly undid the buttons of her blouse. Her shirt fell to the floor, then her bra followed.

As she continued to stroke him, he touched a finger to her nipple and repeatedly flicked it. Her breathing grew labored. She ran a heavy thumb across his engorged head to find it slick with precum. Electricity charged straight to her pulsating clitoris. And every inch of her body tingled.

He seemed in such a hurry to get inside her as he rolled her pants down her legs. "God, you're so pretty, so sexy," he said, stepping from his jeans, leaving them both naked.

She blushed. "I can't wait to become your wife." Her eyes misted. "I'm the happiest woman in the world."

He cupped her neck, pulling it forward. "And I'm the happiest man." He inhaled deeply before thrashing his tongue into her mouth. As their ravenous mouths nipped and sucked and plied away, their hands explored the warmth of each other's naked flesh. Her opening was burning with raw primitive need and her knees felt incredibly weak. She could hardly keep her balance.

Indulging in the heated throes of passion, they wildly fell to the floor, never letting go. She wanted to feel like this forever and always.

"Open wide for me, Sandella." He groaned huskily, looking down at her as she lay on her back. Eager to receive him, she parted her thighs.

He covered her sex with his hot mouth, and nipped her ever so sensitive bud with his sharp teeth. Both pain and pleasure ensued and she winced. As her lids lowered, his deep aroused groans filled her ears.

With driving force, he thrust his tongue inside of her. She flinched. Bucking against his face, she held on hard to his head. "You make me feel so good, Braylon," she panted, curling her toes, heat zapping like fierce fire through her blood. Panting, she dug her nails into his shoulders, then abandoned herself to the overwhelming whirls of pleasant sensations.

"I want you so bad it hurts." He got on his knees then aligned his back up against the wall. The sight of him sitting upright and holding his massive cock in his fist made her mouth water. Starting beneath the deep groove of his round glorious head, the bulging veins of his cock traveled southward and stopped where his hard spheres began. Massaging it up and down, he grazed her arm with his slick tip. "Hop on," he instructed.

My pleasure. She straddled him. She then raised her hips and positioned the opening of her wet sex to his stem .

"Let me just put the head in for a second." Grasping his shoulders, she nodded. Still gripping himself, he circled the hard knob of his erection around the circumference of her pussy. Sparks of desire surged through her tensed body. She slammed down hard on him, and started riding him like an experienced bull rider. He groaned.

She slid back to the top, paused, circled, then crashed down hard into his lap. "Oh yeah, baby." He pecked her neck. "Ride this dick. Fuck me." His large hands rummaged aggressively over her sweating back.

She whimpered repeatedly into his mouth as his thickness scraped her G-spot making her eyes roll heavenward. When she arched her neck backward, he caught a nipple in his hot mouth, and feasted. He then cradled her face and began kissing her everywhere—her face, her throat, her closed eyes.

Their breath was ragged. Their gazes locked.

He swiped her fallen bangs behind her ears. "Do you know what this does to me?" he asked, thrusting her harder.

"I think so."

He cupped her neck and pulled it until their lips lightly touched. "You drive me mad woman."

Certain she was about to explode, she rocked her hips. "Good."

A low growl rumbled inside his throat. His body tensed beneath her. He clenched her hips, rocked, and shot a load of warm semen into her womb. Feeling the strong beats of fluid shooting from the slit of his shaft pushed her over the edge. Biting her bottom lip, she burst with a thunderous orgasm.

"You were incredible," he said, his erection softening inside her flooded crevice.

"So were you." She lay her head on his damp chest, inhaling the strong scent of after-sex lingering in the air.

A long hour later, as Sandella sat on the floor nestled between Braylon's legs chatting about their future together, his cell chirped. "Hello."

"Braylon!" Willa screamed and Sandella could hear her shouting as if she was on the line herself. "Something has come up. You need to come home as quickly as you can."

"What is it, Grandma?"

"Just come see for yourself!" She hung up.

WITH SANDELLA ON HIS HEELS, Braylon stormed through the back door of the estate into the kitchen. "Grandma! Grandma!" he yelled out, searching for her, going crazy out of his mind. What had been so important to the point that she'd demanded he come home immediately?

"I'm in the living room!" Willa shouted.

Braylon hastened toward the living room and when he got there, his heart twisted with rage. *What the fuck!* Disbelieving his fucking eyes, he took a deep breath, then clenched his jaws. Madison Monroe stood next to his grandmother with a smug look on her face.

"Hello, Braylon," she said, jutting her chin.

Braylon didn't need a mirror to know his eyes had narrowed.

"Madison? Why are you here?" His eyes roamed the area for Drayton. He mentally released his breath. *Thank God. He isn't here. Sandella would have a fit. Damn, I should've told her about him before now.*

He turned his gaze to Sandella, then to his frowning grandmother, then back to Madison. His jaw flickered in anger. He crossed his arms over his chest and fought to keep his raging temper from exploding.

Madison stuck out her hand toward Sandella. "Hi, I'm Madison, Braylon's ex. And you are?" Her voice was condescending.

Sandella's smile vanished and a more serious expression took over her features. "What's going on here?"

Madison tossed her straight blond hair behind her shoulder, then crossed her arms over her ample cleavage spilling from her tight, red shirt. She licked her glossy red bottom lip and smiled. "I'm here because—"

The sound of a toy bleeping made Braylon's eyes shift sideways. Coming off the room to his right, Little Drayton entered the living room. The boy gave Braylon a serious once-over, and went and stood beside his mother. Madison ruffled the top of his blond hair.

Drayton was such an adorable little kid. He had fair skin and big, hazel eyes just like him. *Jesus Christ.* I could never deny you if you're mine.

"What's going on?" Sandella's soft voice broke the uncomfortable silence.

"Dear God. You have no clue, do you?" Apparently Madison knew who Sandella was, perhaps from the news of him apprehending her mother's killer.

"What is it that I need to know?"

Braylon's head dropped. He gazed back up at Sandella. His heart ached as he sought the words to tell her. "Drayton may be my son."

Uncertainty developed in her irises, then fury appeared. Braylon felt like someone was choking the hell out of him, and he couldn't breathe.

"There's no maybe in it, Braylon. Drayton is yours," Madison said, pointedly. "Drayton," she patted the little boy's back, "Don't be shy now. Go give your daddy a hug!"

With the tip of his finger between his lips, Drayton slowly walked over to Braylon and glanced up at him with innocent puppy dog eyes. *Dear Lord.* A tender feeling tugged at Braylon's heart. He hefted the kid into his arms.

Grave disappointment settled on Sandella's face. The tear in her right eye was about to fall. "I'll give the three of you some time alone." She briskly walked away.

Willa grabbed her chest, then threw her free hand up and twirled the air. "Lordy Jesus! Have mercy on my soul if this is true." Shaking her head, she quickened away.

Braylon felt like the veins in his neck were about to pop. "You had no right coming here without calling first," Braylon snapped.

Madison strutted up to Braylon. "Now. Now. Don't go getting all mad at me." She rubbed her son's back as he sat perched in Braylon's arms looking shy. She smiled but evil twisted inside her pupils. "I just thought it was high time that Drayton spent some time with his father."

"Aren't you getting ahead of yourself? The paternity results haven't come back yet."

She put her hand on her hip, shifting her weight. "I know for a fact you're the father, Braylon."

"So all that time you and I were apart, you never slept with anyone else?"

She blinked her lashes pitifully. "Do you think I'd actually lie about something like this?" He shrugged. "How insulting."

He looked at Drayton's sweet, baby face. *Maybe she's telling the truth. I mean it'd take a cruel person to lie about the paternity of their child.* "Where are you staying?" he questioned, concerned about where Drayton was laying his head at night.

"I was hoping here."

Oh hell no! Grandma would never go for that. "Until the paternity results become available, I'll put you and Drayton up at the Marriott."

"The Marriott!" she huffed.

"I'll get you a big suite, the best there is."

She caressed his arm in a flirtatious way. "Thanks, baby."

He handed her Drayton. "I need to go speak with Sandella. After I'm done, I'll take you to the hotel."

She bestowed him with a smile which looked phony. "Please don't take long, Braylon. We miss you." He went in search of the love of his life.

Braylon glared out the kitchen window and spotted Sandella standing on the boat dock gazing out at the river. *I done fucked up! She'll never forgive me for keeping this from her.* After he mustered up the courage to go speak with her, he hoofed it across the lawn.

As he made his way toward her the cool breeze bristled his cheeks while sailing over his scalp. A sudden roar of thunder echoed in his ears. *It's about to pour.*

He approached Sandella from behind and put a palm to her shoulder. "Sandella." When she turned and captured his gaze, his heart shattered like glass. Her face was soaked from crying. He felt his head spinning as he looked down at her. "I'm so sorry, baby," he said.

"How old is he?" She wiped the tear falling from her left eye. "Three."

The thunderous sounds of the weather exploding around them caused her to jump. She sniffed. "He's beautiful. How long have you known about him?"

God, it killed him to see her in this pain. *What a fool I am for hurting her like this. She deserves better.* A single drop of rain collided with his forehead.

When he went to pull her up against his chest, she slapped his hands away. "Don't touch me," she spat out. She blinked and another tear fell. "Just answer the question."

Guilt knotted his gut. "I found out about Drayton right before I arrived here."

Her hands flung upward. "And you didn't tell me?" She sighed. "Didn't you think you should've told me this before I slept with you? Huh? Huh?" She gnawed her bottom lip.

Regret filled him. "Yes. I should've told you, but I'm not sure if he's even mine."

Her eyes spread wide with confusion. "What do you mean?" She ran a hand over her dripping nose.

"Madison didn't tell me about Drayton until after I returned home. It was only a few weeks ago that she finally agreed to a paternity test. I'm waiting as we speak for the results."

She shook her head. "I can see it in your eyes." She turned her gaze toward the river.

He curled his hands around her biceps. "Tell me…what do you see in my eyes?"

Shaking her head, she steadied those big sad eyes on him. "I can see in your eyes that you're going to leave me if he's yours…aren't you?"

He released the steely grip he had on her and let his arms fall to his sides. *She knows me so well.* As light drizzles of rain pecked his scalp, his hands went to his hips and he briefly transferred his eyes to the river, then back to her sorrowful glare. How could he do this to her? he wondered, the sound of rain pounding inside his ears.

"Oh God, you are! Why did you ask me to marry you if you

knew this could happen?" she wailed.

Hard sheets of rain fell from the sky.

"You should've never asked me to marry you, Braylon. Never!"

He'd never said he was smart when it came to making decisions regarding love. "I guess I asked you to be my wife because I just love you so much. And, truthfully, as awful as it may sound, I'm praying that little precious boy in there isn't mine." It broke him down to admit such ugly thing. But that's just how much he loved her. Besides, his relationship with Sandella was much stronger than his was with Drayton.

Thunder boomed.

Lightning cracked the sky.

Rain pounded down harder over their bodies.

"I guess we'll just have to wait and see what the outcome is...won't we? Please...don't call me until you know the results." She slid the ring off her trembling finger. Giving him a brutal stare, she slapped it into his open hand, then took off running toward the estate.

Holding the ring in his fist, his heart wrenched as she fled. "Sandella! Come back! Don't leave like this!" *Damn.* For the first time in his life, he felt like crying over a woman. When he attempted to run after her, he slipped and fell on the dock. With his hands flattened on the wet wood, he lolled his head back and let the rain connect with his face, hoping it would wipe away the pain.

Chapter Sixteen

BRAYLON STOOD ON THE DECK of his home in Harbor Island gazing out at his backyard. The emerald grass was in need of a good mowing. And the big bushy hedges were in dire need of trimming. With everything that had been going on, he hadn't had time to tend to it.

When he looked out over the glistening water, the sweet remembrance of the night he and Sandella had taken a boat ride in Drake's boat sailed inside his brain. They'd made love on the campgrounds that night. She'd sat in his lap and ridden him backward.

Missing her dearly, his chest tightened. He turned, pulled open the sliding glass door, and stepped inside. Sandella should be here with him decorating this big house he'd purchased with her in mind, and the three or four kids he hoped they'd one day share. *I need to hear her voice.* He slid his cell from his clip, and dialed Sandella.

"Hello," she answered, and the sweet sound of her soft voice melted his heart, made his shaft threaten to swell.

He walked into the kitchen and sat down in the chair at the

dinette table, the only piece of furniture he had. "I miss you," he admitted, dying to see her, aching to make sweet love to her.

"Do you have the paternity results yet?" she asked pointedly.

"No. Not yet."

"I can't do this, Braylon. I wish I could, but I can't. I'm sorry." She ended the call without saying goodbye.

Damn! He dropped his head in his hands. As he sat there moping, the doorbell rang. *Who could that be?* he wondered, trekking through the living room. When he pulled the door open to find Madison and Drayton on his porch, the knots in his shoulders deepened. Not because of innocent Drayton, but because of the scheming Madison.

Madison's blond hair was curled in loose ringlets today. Wearing a purple, tight sweater dress and a pair of five-inch heels, she actually looked pretty. She'd always reminded him of Marilyn Monroe. Too bad her outside didn't match her inside.

Holding Drayton's hand, she held onto a long cylinder-shaped roll of something with the other. "Good morning."

"Good morning. Come in." He stepped to the side, and after she entered he shut the door. Last night she'd called him and said she had something important to tell him. With that being said, he'd given her his address, and told her she could stop by this morning. Perhaps she wanted to talk about Drayton and how they'd raise him. Or perhaps she came to say that Drayton wasn't his. *Perhaps.*

"Come, this way." He headed toward the kitchen.

Her eyes wandered over the spacious areas. "My, my, my...this is some place you have."

"Thanks."

He came to a stop in front of the kitchen table. "So what did you want to talk to me about that you couldn't tell me over the phone?"

"I'd rather show you than tell you." She removed the paper

from beneath her armpit and rolled it out on the table. It was light blue wallpaper with white clouds as the background. "I thought this would look great in your guest bathroom."

Jesus Christ. She's got to be kidding me or fucking crazy. No, she's both. "Excuse me?"

"Yeah. I went online and pulled up photos of your home. You know you can do that, right?"

"Yes, Madison. I'm fully aware."

"Oh. Okay. As I was saying…after looking at your house online, I saw how bland it looked. So I went to Lowe's and picked this up." Her eyes drifted to the wallpaper then back up at him. "You do want Drayton and me to move in here, right? Isn't that the plan?" Silence. Silence. "I just assumed—"

"Yes. Madison. Drayton can come live with me once I get the results and know he's mine for sure." A vivid picture of his father walking out on him flashed across his mind.

Her face split into a grin and she threw her arms around him. She nestled her cheek into the juncture of his chest like a kitten snuggling up against its mother. "I knew you'd do the right thing by us. I just knew you would." The doorbell rang again. She pried her arms from him. "I need to go get my nails done. Can you please watch Drayton until I get back?"

"Sure. No problem." *Sandella should be decorating this house, not her.*

She stooped down in front of Drayton. "Daddy's going to watch you until I get back. Okay?"

"But, I want to go with you," he whined.

"Mommy has to run and do things that only girls can do. So be a big boy and stay here with your daddy." She pinched his cheek causing it to turn apple red. "Okay?"

Braylon lifted Drayton in his arms. "How about you and I go fishing or to the park and play football later?"

Drayton's eyes lit like shining stars. "Yeeeyyy! Football. I like football! But I don't know how to fish."

She kissed his forehead, and headed for the front door. Halfway there, the doorbell rang again. It was Willa and Drake. My, wasn't he blessed to have so many visitors this morning? Willa, Drake, and Madison acknowledged one another. A few seconds later, Madison hopped in the car and backed out of the driveway.

Barely inside the house, Willa asked, "How she gone leave this boy with you and he don't even know you?" she started. Before Braylon could respond, she said, "He doesn't look anything like you. Well, he does have your eyes. But that don't mean a thing. I bet he ain't yo—"

Braylon shook his head. "Grandma. Not in front of him."

Willa touched Drayton's arm. "Baby, who's your real daddy?" she asked, ignoring Braylon.

Drayton pointed. "He is! We're going to play football!"

The adults gathered inside the kitchen around the table while Drayton sat in the family room playing with the toys Madison had stored inside his backpack.

"Would y'all like something to drink?" Braylon offered, sitting at the table with his grandparents.

"No. We're good," she answered for both her and Drake. She then placed her hand on top of his. "I know you want to do what's best for Drayton if it turns out that he's your son. But, if you're not happy, your son won't be happy. That child will see it in your eyes if you're miserable. You don't have to commit to Madison in order to raise your son. Now I know you didn't ask for my advice, but I'm gone give it to you anyway—you need to keep your promise to Sandella and marry her."

"Now ain't that the truth!" Drake said. "Sandella has been like a daughter to us. She's a beautiful person...inside and out. They don't make them like her anymore. And Madison, well," Drake patted his chest, "something just don't sit right in here with me when it comes to that girl."

Braylon's mind once again flashed back to the day his father had walked out on him. He'd left his mother and his siblings for another woman, and it'd nearly destroyed them all. He didn't want to ever bring a child of his pain like he'd experienced. So leaving Drayton wouldn't be an option if he was his son. He just couldn't do it.

"I agree with you both. Sandella is the perfect woman for me. I love her more than anything in this world. But if Drayton is my son, then I'm going to raise him in a home with a mother and a father. I will never leave him like my father left me."

"So your mind's made up?" Drake said.

"Yes, it is."

Willa stood. "Apparently your mind is made up and there's nothing I can do to change it. But just know I had a dream last night about fish." Her brows hiked.

"What do fish have to do with anything?" he asked, pushing his chair back, then standing. He glanced back over his shoulder at Drayton, who was now coloring. When he returned his gaze back to his grandmother a big smile was plastered on her face.

"When a person dreams about fish, it means someone close to them is pregnant. All my girlfriends have hit menopause so it's not one of them. The only other person close to me that can remotely be pregnant is Sandella." She shrugged. "Looks to me you done got yourself in a mighty fine mess here."

Drake chortled. "Stop with all those myths, Willa, and let's go."

For the first time in days a light chuckle escaped Braylon's lips. "Grandma, you are too funny. I don't believe in those old wives' tales."

"It's gone be true. You just wait and see," she laughed, making her way toward the front door.

Braylon crossed in front of Willa to open the door and found an African-American mailman standing in his doorway. "I have a certified letter for Braylon Wexler."

"That's me." The bald-headed gentleman handed him the letter and Braylon signed his name on the electronic device. "Thanks."

The young man nodded. "You're welcome, sir. Have a great day."

Braylon's pulse thudded wildly in his neck as he examined the envelope from the Diagnostic Laboratory Clinic containing the paternity results regarding little Drayton. The last time he'd spoken with the clinic, they'd stated it might take another week before he received them because Madison had taken her sweet precious time getting Drayton tested. But now, finally, here they were.

Nervous, he inhaled deeply. The contents inside would determine his fate with Sandella—a woman he adored. Would he end up marrying the woman he loved? The woman that made his heart swell with love and bubble over with joy? Or would he end up with Madison only for the sake of raising his son?

Can I really stomach a life with Madison knowing my heart belongs to Sandella? Maybe Grandma is right, being with Madison just for the sake of Drayton will be a disaster.

"What's wrong?" Willa asked, forcing him to snap out of his daydream.

"These are the paternity results."

Impatience developed in Willa's voice. "Well, don't just stand there. Hurry up and open it." She put her hands on her hips.

Drake cleared his throat. "Maybe you should read the results when you're alone."

Willa waved off his suggestion and shook her head. "Stop speaking such nonsense, Drake. What better time for him to do it than when he's with us, his family?"

Braylon's fingers trembled as he broke the seal of the sturdy envelope. Inhaling a ragged breath, he pulled out the sheet of paper and let it rest in his hand before reading it. With his heart slamming against his rib cage like a sledgehammer, his eyes darted from his grandpa to his grandmother. *Just read the damn results.* Finally, he brought the paper up to his eyes.

"So, what does it say?" Willa's impatience was getting the best of her.

"Shhh," Drake encouraged.

Braylon felt his mouth twist angrily. As he reread the patterning results his eyes narrowed. Madison had lied! *That no good, scheming woman!* He hated thinking of any woman as the "b" word, but damn, that's what she behaved like. How could she do this to him? Better yet, how could she do this to her own son, that wonderful kid sitting in his family room playing with his toys?

She'd gone to such great lengths so she could live the lifestyle of a rich wife. Well, her attempt to get her hands on the Wexlers' fortune had failed her and rightfully so.

His blood boiled through his veins. "He's not mine. Madison lied." He shoved the paper to Willa and could feel his nostrils flaring.

"I knew it!" Willa shouted after reading the negative report. "I knew that precious child wasn't yours all along. She's a gold digger."

Drake's eyebrows dipped. "Say what? Drayton's not yours?" Willa passed the paper to Drake so he could read it, too. "Well, I'll be damned. I've seen some low-down dirty women in my lifetime, but this whore takes the cake."

Willa folded her arms over her breasts. "Some women will do anything for money."

Braylon's temper rose to the point of no return. "Grandma, Grandpa, if you don't mind, I need to be alone when Madison returns."

Willa and Drake assented, then left. Braylon marched into the family room where Drayton was still playing. He crouched down beside him to place a kiss on his forehead. A part of him was disappointed to learn this innocent child wasn't his. But the other half of him was glad, because now he and Sandella could marry and have the life they both wanted.

Torn with conflicting emotions, he pulled Drayton against his chest. *Your mother was wrong for putting you through this. She deceived us all.* "I'm so sorry. I really am."

Drayton peered up at him with those big squirrel eyes of his. "What's wrong, Daddy?"

Braylon's heart squeezed.

BRAYLON STOOD ON THE DOCK in his backyard taking in the beautiful sight of the sun shining on the river. He reached down and grabbed the fishing pole from the wooden planks, then steadied it over his shoulder. "You swing it like this, sport." He tossed the line into the water hoping the fishing excursion might help to quell the burning anger brewing inside him. Madison was in for a rude awakening when she returned.

"Can I try, Daddy? Can I fish, too?" Drayton asked, yanking on his pant leg.

Braylon gazed down at poor Drayton. Just when he was getting used to the idea that the boy might be his son, he'd found out he wasn't. God, he wanted a child, but not like this. "Sure you can fish." He lifted him into his arms, perched him on the wooden railing, then guided his hands to grip the pole. With his big hands covering Drayton's tiny ones, his mind drifted back to what his grandmother had said. She'd dreamed of fish.

Pleasant fantasies of Sandella carrying his child brought a wide smile to his face. And for the first time in hours the brutal anger he'd harbored started lifting from his discontented soul. God, he'd love it if she was pregnant. Considering the notion was highly unlikely, he pushed the idea to the back of his mind.

Drayton's lips curled upward. "I like fishing, Daddy!"

Braylon cringed. *She even trained him to call me Daddy. How conniving.* "Me too. I'm glad you—"

"There're my two favorite boys in the whole wide world!" Madison shouted from the deck of the patio.

"Mommy!" Drayton's soft giggles melted Braylon's heart.

He gathered the child in his arms, dropped the rod on the dock, and strode toward Madison as she stood waving in the distance. *She has to leave Hilton Head today. I mean today!* When he reached her, she gazed up at him and settled a soft hand to his cheek. The muscle in his jaw flickered. Thank God Drayton was there because if he weren't, there was no telling what he'd do.

"Thanks for watching him for me. I had a wonderful time getting to know the area. I'm going to love it here. I was thinking, for Drayton's sake, it'd be best if we move in right away. While I'm thankful for the hotel, it's just too small. And he's used to a much bigger space."

Braylon tightly curled his hand around her wrist and lowered her arm to her side. "Please keep your hands to yourself."

She blinked, deception contorting the features of her face. "What's gotten into you?" she asked, tilting her head.

"Drayton, go inside and play with your toys," he suggested.

"But I want to stay with you and Mommy."

"I need to speak with your mommy alone. Okay?" He slid back the patio door and after Drayton entered, he closed it behind him. "How dare you?"

Stark fear darkened Madison's pupils. "How dare I what?" She played dumb quite well.

"I received the paternity results today. And guess what they revealed?"

Diverting her gaze sideways, she scratched the back of her neck. "Today? I thought they wouldn't be ready for another week or two. I just gave them the blood sample before coming here." She chuckled. "I hope they didn't rush them and make a mistake."

Liar! He clutched her shoulders. "Stop it," he barked through clenched teeth. "You lied. The paternity results confirmed Drayton is not mine."

Tears welled up in her eyes then started rolling down her bright red face. "Yes, he is yours. If the results came out negative, they're wrong." She swiped at the tears trailing down both cheeks.

He huffed. "Of course they came out negative...Madison... because he's not my son."

"No. Don't say that. He's your son. This has to be a mistake," she cried.

Gritting his molars, he put his hands on his hips, closed his eyes, and counted until his temper tamped down. When he reopened his eyes, he couldn't stand the sight of her. "I tell you what. I know a very reputable doctor here...let's drive to his office right now and have another paternity test done. I'll call him right now to see if he's available," he stated, entering the number on his phone.

"Good afternoon. Dr. LeRoux's office."

"Good afternoon. This is Braylon Wexler calling for Dr. LeRoux. I'd like to make an app—"

Madison's hand flew up to grab her head. "Okay. Okay. He may not be yours."

Braylon tapped the screen on the cell without saying goodbye, ending the call. Infuriated, he said. "There's no maybe in it, Madison. You outright lied!"

She cried, "I didn't lie, Braylon. I honestly thought he might be yours." She wiped the drips running from her bright red nose.

Infuriated, he hiked his brows. "You thought he *might* be mine?

Really? *Might be mine*." He signaled quotation marks with his fingers to emphasize the *might*.

She sniffled. "Yes. It was between you and one other guy."

"Just one, huh?" He pinched the bridge of his nose feeling an intense pain jabbing his temples. "So...since you knew I had a fifty-fifty chance of being Drayton's father, you just decided to put two sticks in a can and draw?" He stepped closer to her, his heart writhing with disgust. "Or did you select me because you wanted to live the fancy lifestyle you thought you'd get from marrying into a wealthy family?" He wiped a hand down his face.

"I'm sorry. I was hoping once you got to know him it wouldn't matter whether he was your son or not."

Jesus Christ! Braylon looked beyond a weeping Madison into the family room. When his gaze landed on Drayton sitting on the floor looking back at him, his heart softened. "Look...Drayton is a great kid, and I actually like the little fella...a lot. But he needs to develop a relationship with his real father. Now, if you'll excuse me, I have someone I need to go see."

"Who, Sandella? She'll never love you like I do, Braylon. Never."

Braylon pulled the sliding glass door open. "Please, Madison... do us all a favor and just leave."

SITTING IN THE CAR, SANDELLA swung her feet to the asphalt and slid out. After she closed the car door, she paused and took in the sight of the beige, one-story building in front of her. Although this building was where she temporarily housed SugarKanes, perhaps after her building on the ocean was finished, and *if* she continued growing, she could purchase this building and turn it into a small, eclectic Southern diner.

Tears wet her eyes. Hurt gripped her heart. *If it hadn't been for Braylon, none of this would've ever happened. I miss him. It makes no sense for him to end his relationship with me just because he has a son. Why me?*

She kicked at a pebble lying in the gravel, then began making her way to the front of the store. Struggling to hold back the cry dying to escape her, she clambered the steps. As she unlocked the door, a cool breeze rolled off the ocean from across the street and pricked her scalp. When she entered the bakery, the sweet smell of freshly baked pistachio muffins crept up her nose.

"Good morning, Taylor," she said warmly as she passed the glass cases displaying assorted desserts.

Taylor smiled, then slid a fresh caramel pecan pie into the case. "Good morning, Sandella. Last night after you left, we got a huge order for an anniversary party."

She paused in her tracks. "How huge?"

"They need a cake that feeds five hundred people."

"Five hundred people! For who?"

"Richmond Spaulding."

Sandella gasped. While she'd never had the opportunity to meet the wealthy millionaire, Richmond Spaulding, she'd heard an awful lot of nice things about him. At one point he was the most eligible bachelor in this small town and throughout the states. Although he was happily married, the women in Hilton Head Island were constantly throwing themselves at him, or at least vying for his attention.

"When's the anniversary party?"

"In three weeks."

"Three weeks!"

Taylor nodded. "Mr. Spaulding's wife wants you to come by the home, that's if you can, for a consultation."

"I'd be more than happy to go meet with her. I'll call her later to schedule an appointment." Sandella perused the small sitting area for her customers, then as she headed toward her office a wave of nausea churned in her stomach.

Entering her office should provide her with a sense of peace, pride, and joy, she thought, closing the door behind her. But considering she didn't have Braylon to celebrate with, the only thing she felt was sadness. She flopped down on the peach leather couch adjacent to her desk and rubbed a hand over her belly.

What if I'm pregnant? She separated the flaps of her purse, reached inside, and pulled out the early pregnancy test. For weeks now she hadn't been feeling herself, but had chalked it up to her horrible situation involving Braylon and Madison. However, now, with her period two weeks late, she'd finally stopped by the drugstore on her way to work this morning and gotten the darn test. *If I'm pregnant, I'm not going to tell him. I don't want him with me just because I'm pregnant.* She sighed. *That's dumb to even think such a thing. He wanted me before, and had asked me to marry him. He loves me. I can feel it in my heart.*

Just as Sandella stood to go take the pregnancy test, her desk phone rang. She tossed the test back into her purse. "Hello." It was Taylor.

"Mr. Spaulding is on the other line and he wants to know if you can come by his house this morning to speak with his fiancée, Salina."

Getting a big business opportunity like this brought a cheerful smile to her face. "Please put him through to me."

By the time Sandella had ended her phone call with Mr. Spaulding and the morning rush crowd had come and gone, it was high noon and she was exhausted. She told Taylor to hold her calls, kicked off her shoes, and plopped down on the sofa to relax. With her elbow propped up on the edge of the sofa, her nipples felt sore, and her eyelids began drifting.

Braylon hovered over Sandella while she lay with her back

pressed into the cushions of the couch. As heat swarmed inside her love canal, she spied the door and noticed she'd failed to lock it. Dear Lord, what if Taylor or one of her other employees walked in on her and Braylon about to make sweet love? "Braylon, wait," she moaned.

He eagerly zipped down his jeans. "I've waited long enough." He yanked her skirt up to her hips, pushed her panties to the side, and inserted two of his big fingers into her opening.

"We can't. Not in here," she moaned, pressing her pubic bone against his tormenting hand and causing his fingers to slip deeper.

"I want you. Now. And I'm not taking no for an answer. I've missed your sweet, delicate pussy, Sandella." His sensual words stirred her, aroused her, made her wetter.

Unable to refuse his request, she parted her quaking thighs and let herself sink into the whirlwind of pleasure he bestowed her with. He crushed his mouth into hers, then slid his tongue to the back of her throat. As his thick fingers plunged her essence, their tongues curled and lapped and sucked. It'd been so long, too long, since she'd felt his dominating male physique on top of her and his sheathed cock grinding her belly.

Sweat saturated her back, and oh...oh...oh, Goooddd! Her breathing heightened. Just as she was about to come, he pulled his fingers from her entrance, sniffed them, then one by one he sucked off her creamy fluid.

He reached inside his pants and pulled out his heavily veined shaft. The engorged head looked delicious and made her mouth water. "Do you miss this?" he asked, fisting the beast. He grazed her arm with his steely tool. Tremors of delight pimpled her arms and her nipples snapped into tight buds.

"Yes, baby. I miss you, so much, baby. Please, please," she begged, writhing with the need to be fucked by him. "Please make love to me."

"I miss you too, baby." He dropped hard kisses on her forehead, then plunged deep inside her wet cunt.

Arching his back, he stroked...and stroked...and stroked her deliciously.

As his massive cock stretched her walls bringing her sheer pleasure, she dug her nails into his back. A few moments later a shallow cry rolled off her tongue and she exploded around the thick circumference of his stroking member.

Bam! Bam! Bam!

"Sandella. Wake up. Look outside."

Sandella's eyes fluttered open. Slouching on the sofa, she crossed her legs and felt herself having an orgasm. Her sensitive womb was shattering into a million pieces. She rolled her head backward and cupped her opened mouth. "Ahhhh!"

"Hurry up or you're going to miss it!" Taylor shouted.

"Miss what?" She flung open the door.

Taylor ran over to the window and opened the blinds. She pointed up at the sky. "That!"

When Sandella gazed up at the sky, her breath caught in her throat. "Oh my God!" A jet was flying high in the sky writing a message. It read: *Sandella, will you marry me?* "I don't understand. I—"

"I love you," came the deep voice from behind.

She whirled to find Braylon standing in her office looking just as sexy now as he had a few moments ago in her dream, her wet dream. The black cotton shirt he wore snugged tightly against his ripped chest muscles, and the black denim jeans did little to hide the knot pressing against his zipper.

"Braylon." His name slipped softly from her lips. What was he doing here in the flesh? She tried hard not to get her hopes up.

"Taylor, I'd like to speak with Sandella alone."

With a huge smile displaying at the corners of her mouth,

Taylor nodded then flew out of the room.

Braylon shut the door. "I got the results back from the paternity test," he said, getting straight to the point. "He's not mine."

She sucked in a deep breath. "Are you sure?"

"I wouldn't have asked you to marry me again if I wasn't. I'm so sorry, baby, for keeping the truth from you. I was wrong for doing that, but my love, I didn't want to hurt you until I was certain." He got down on one knee, reached in his pocket, and presented her with the diamond he'd given her while at the house a few weeks ago. "Again, will you marry me?"

"I think I'm pregnant," she blurted.

His eyes stretched wide. "Grandma said that you were."

"She did? But I didn't tell her. I haven't told anyone. I haven't even taken the test to confirm it yet. How did she know?"

He chuckled. "She said she had a dream about fish which means someone close to you is pregnant. You're the only person she could think of." He looked down at the ring, then recaptured her face. "Are you going to answer the question? I want you to marry me, and I promise, I'll never hurt you again."

The mere fact that Braylon had been willing to leave her if Drayton was his disturbed her, and she fought hard to bring herself to grips with the fact. But considering his past with his father had once nearly destroyed him a part of her had to understand. "So you promise you'll never hurt me again."

"I swear. You have my word. Just say you'll marry me, baby. I'm begging you to take me back."

A soft whimper escaped her. "Yes. I'll marry you, Braylon." He slid the ring up her finger. She looked up at the ceiling and let the tears slip from her eyes.

He stood and cradled her wet face in his large hands. "I can't wait to share the rest of my life with you. Now let's go to the store to get a pregnancy test."

"I already have one in my purse."

"Let's take it now."

She nodded. She walked over to her desk drawer, reached into her purse, and grabbed the pregnancy test.

Three minutes later, Sandella came out of the restroom, smiling.

"So what are the results?"

She placed a hand on her stomach. "I'm pregnant. Are you sure you can handle a new wife with mood swings?"

Braylon's face split into a happy grin. He strode over to her, draped an arm around her waist, and kissed her lips. "Not only am I sure about you and the baby, but I'm ready to begin my life with you. I want you to move in with me, today. Will you please do that for me and for him?" He lowered a flat palm to her belly.

"What makes you think it's a boy?"

"Because, baby, the Wexler men are known for their dominant *y* chromosomes." He now placed both his hands on her belly and held her to his chest like he never planned on letting her go.

Epilogue

Fourth of July

Nine Months Later

SANDELLA STOOD AT THE SLIDING glass door of her Victorian style home in Harbor Island admiring the beauty of her backyard. The hot sun shined down on the glistening river. A white luxury yacht sailed by, making its way toward Hilton Head Island. Barbeque-scented smoke spiraled from the grill up into the summer air. The day seemed perfect, she thought, beaming in delight.

As Braylon stood on the wooden deck of their home grilling shrimp, chicken, ribs, and steak, she pulled back the sliding glass door, strolled through the patio, and stopped when she reached the middle of the deck. Making an effort to fashion him a pretty smile, she caressed the swell of her protruding pregnant belly. "Sonny just arrived," she said, referring to Braylon's middle brother.

Braylon's face lit up as he returned her smile. He lowered the cover on the grill, walked up to Sandella, and slipped his tongue into her mouth. As she savored the salty flavor rolling off his tongue, her body tingled with need. *Mmmm.* She could never get enough of her husband.

"I can't wait to eat your pussy after they leave," he breathed against her soft, sweet lips.

Laughing against his mouth, she playfully hit his arm. "Do you ever think of anything else?" she asked, loving the man she'd married.

"Yes."

"What?"

"Getting you pregnant, over...and over...and over again. As soon as you pop this one out," he rubbed circles over her full belly, "and after you get your six-week checkup, I want to start trying again."

Smiling, she fisted her hips. "Six weeks?"

He nodded. "Yes."

"Get in here you two lovebirds!" Her brother, Aric, shouted from the kitchen.

Sandella's heart filled with joy when she and Braylon entered their formal dining room to find Willa, Drake, Royce, her brothers, her father, and the rest of the Wexler men crowded around the long, rectangular table. Everything looked so festive.

A square cake with fireworks was centered on the table. Red, white, and blue balloons floated to the ceilings. And Fourth of July plates, napkins, and cups decorated the side table.

"Where's Caroline?" Braylon probed.

Aric confirmed, "Oh, she and Chandler went horseback riding."

Braylon's brows dipped. "I hope Chandler's not trying to make a move on my baby sister."

Kane squinted. "Why not? You made a move on his."

The room filled with laughter.

Suddenly, a sharp pain sliced through Sandella's midsection. She grabbed her belly as her spine curved. She took a deep breath.

Braylon put a gentle hand on her lower spine. "Are you okay?"

Releasing a breath, she nodded. "Yes. I think I'm having Braxton-Hicks."

A wide smile developed on Kane's face. "I'm gone be a grand-father soon. Hot damn!"

LATER ON THAT EVENING BRAYLON stood in the family room at the foot of the staircase peering up to the second level. "Hurry up, Sandella," he yelled out, "it's time to light the fireworks." The rest of the crew was outside anxiously awaiting for the show to begin. To make this a night to remember, he'd purchased sparklers, firecrackers, and assorted fireworks.

Sandella's hand glided along the black railing as she slowly descended the staircase. When she finally reached him, the corners of her eyes crinkled. She gasped. She clenched the sides of her belly. "I think it's—" Water gushed from her center, down her legs, to the carpet. "I'm in labor," she said, panting harshly.

His heart spun. "I'm going to get the bag." He scampered up the staircase, grabbed the baby bag sitting in the corner, then darted back downstairs to where she now stood breathing sporadically.

"Ahhh!" she bellowed, perspiration dotting her forehead. With one hand on the rail, she clamped his arm. Her knees buckled. "It hurts so bad," she cried, "I don't think I can walk."

"Sonny! Chandler! Aric!" Braylon yelled for his brother and brothers-in-law.

Sonny and Aric charged inside the room. "Jesus Christ!" Aric said. "Is she in labor?"

Braylon nodded. "Help me get her in the car."

Aric and Braylon lifted Sandella off her feet. When they opened the front door, all of their family members stood out in the front yard looking excited. Kane wheeled up to the Hummer with a big smile on his face. "Somebody get the god damn door!" He patted his shirt pocket. "Damn, I done ran out of cigarettes!"

Sonny flung open the rear door, and the men slid Sandella onto the seat. Braylon jogged around to the driver's side, hopped in, and just as he put the car in reverse, the black stallions carrying Chandler and Caroline came galloping up in the driveway. Colorful fireworks erupted in the dark sky overhead as Braylon sped away from the beautiful scene, his heart palpitating wildly in his chest.

AT ELEVEN FIFTY-NINE ON the evening of July fourth, a beautiful baby girl named Logan Caroline Wexler was born. As Sandella sat upright in the hospital bed, her physician eased her darling daughter into her arms. Feeling extremely blessed, she cradled her baby against her bosom then kissed her forehead.

Braylon stood over her bed smiling down at her and Logan. "She's beautiful just like you," he said, gently swiping Sandella's errant bangs matted to her forehead in with the rest of her damp hair. He then trailed a finger over her cheek. "Thank you for giving me this precious little angel. You've made me the happiest man on earth." He bent down to kiss her cheek.

She glanced up at Braylon, tears wetting her eyes. "This is the best day of my life. Well, one of the best days. Marrying you is the other."

"Mine too." He slid his hand in his pocket, pulled out a white velvet bag, reached in, then extracted a beautiful sterling silver bracelet. Holding the expensive piece of jewelry up, he let it dangle in the air before her eyes. "This is for you," he said, circling it around her wrist.

Admiring the keepsake, she twisted her wrist to get a good look at the pink diamond charm attached to it. It was a baby shoe. "Thanks. I love it." His eyes gleamed. "Every time you give me a baby, I'm going to add a different charm to your bracelet.

Hopefully, you'll end up with at least five."

Five would be fine with her, she thought, a single tear streaming down her face. "I guess I'll be getting started in six weeks."

"Now that's what I wanted to hear." Braylon reached for his daughter, then held her against his muscular chest.

As Sandella looked on in merriment, she knew she had so much to be thankful for. For starters, the man standing beside her bed holding her daughter loved her. On top of that, this same man had gone to dangerous lengths to find her mother's killer. And also because of him, her business SugarKanes was profiting millions, had its own building in Hilton Head Island, and had gone national.

How she'd ever gotten this lucky was beyond her. The only thing she knew for sure was: she'd done herself some good by— *Marrying the Marine*.

the end

Dear Readers,
Thanks a million for reading *Marrying the Marine*. I hope you enjoyed reading the book just as much as I enjoyed writing it. Reviews, comments, and likes are greatly appreciated. If you have a quick moment, please write an honest review for Marrying the Marine on the retailer's site where you purchased it.
Fondly,
Sabrina

Also, if you enjoyed the book, please remember you can share it with a friend via the lending feature. In addition, you can help readers find it by recommending it to friends and family, reading and discussion groups, online forums, etc.

ABOUT THE AUTHOR

Sabrina Sims McAfee is your writer of women's fiction, romantic suspense, and contemporary romance. She loves writing about strong men, and sexy strong women, and the adventurous journeys they travel. She lived in Florida for most of her life, but now she's a current resident of Myrtle Beach, SC. She lives there with her husband and two teenage children. In her leisure she likes spending time with her family, reading, traveling, and watching reality and suspense TV shows.

Sabrina's goal is to someday produce one of her books into a movie. As she strives toward her dream, she plans to study the craft of writing, take writing risks, and try her hardest to bring her readers great satisfying stories.

She loves hearing from her readers so please feel free to email her at Sabrina@sabrinasimsmcafee.com or visit her online at www.sabrinasimsmcafee.com

Made in the USA
Lexington, KY
11 August 2015